Robert Jackson was born in 1941 and educated at Richmond School, Yorkshire. He has been a full-time author since 1969, specializing in aviation and military history. During his life he has travelled extensively, and he speaks five languages; he has flown a wide variety of aircraft, ranging from jets to gliders. He is a recently retired member of the Royal Air Force Volunteer Reserve, and is currently working on the eighth book in the Yeoman series.

Also by Robert Jackson

TARGET TOBRUK
MALTA VICTORY
SQUADRON SCRAMBLE
HURRICAN SQUADRON
MOSQUITO SQUADRON
OPERATION DIVER
FIGHTER ACES OF WORLD WAR II

and published by Corgi Books

Tempest Squadron
Yeoman in the Battle of the Ardennes

Robert Jackson

CORGI BOOKS

TEMPEST SQUADRON

A CORGI BOOK 0 552 12148 7

Originally published in Great Britain by Arthur Barker Limited

PRINTING HISTORY

Arthur Barker edition published 1981
Corgi edition published 1983

This book is set in 10/11 Plantin

Corgi Books are published by
Transworld Publishers Ltd.,
Century House, 61–63 Uxbridge Road,
Ealing, London W5 5SA

Made and printed in Great Britain by
Cox & Wyman Ltd, Reading

1

The pilot of the twin-engined Avro Anson gave a gaping yawn, a compound of boredom and tiredness, and peered down at a fragment of Belgian landscape that appeared momentarily through the ragged veil of stratus cloud. That single glimpse was sufficient; he had no need to check his map to find out where he was, for he had come to know this bit of Europe like the back of his hand.

Three or four times every week, the Anson pilot made the same tedious run from Redhill, in Surrey, to Eindhoven in Holland, carrying mail, laundry, fresh clothing, whisky, soap and other odds and ends that combined to make life just bearable for the pilots of the Spitfires, Typhoons and Tempests belonging to the squadrons of the RAF's No. 83 Group. He and the other men who flew the lumbering Ansons of No. 83 Group Support Unit also brought frequent batches of replacement pilots, for the Group's losses in action were heavy. Idly, he wondered about the five men who now sat behind him, shivering with cold despite their flying jackets as they huddled in the Anson's vibrating fuselage. Four of them looked too young to be out of school, while the fifth . . .

The Anson pilot shuddered inwardly. The fifth man had, at some time, suffered appalling burns; his face was a mass of scar tissue out of which two dark eyes shone like live coals, burning with some indefinable emotion. Below the eyes, a shapeless lump might have passed for a nose, while the mouth was a white slit surrounded by lesions.

The burned man was a flight lieutenant, and below his pilot's wings he wore the ribbon of the DFM, an indication that he must once have been a non-commissioned officer. His hair was snowy white, but it was impossible to guess at his age. Whatever story of suffering lay behind that mask-like face, the Anson pilot thought, the man must be crazy to be going back into action again after what he had obviously been through.

No. 83 Group was right in the thick of the fighting in November 1944, operating from advanced airfields in Holland in support of Field-Marshal Montgomery's Northern Group of Armies as they drove on doggedly towards Germany. The Germans were resisting ferociously and there was bitter fighting every step of the way, as the men of the 1st Canadian Army had found to their cost when, at the beginning of November, they had stormed the fortress island of Walcheren – still defended by the Germans and commanding the approaches to the vital port of Antwerp – in the wake of a terrific air and naval bombardment.

Only after nine days of savage fighting had the last Germans on Walcheren surrendered, and the ferocity of the battle had brought the total of Canadian casualties, in their 2nd Division alone, to almost four thousand in five weeks.

On 8 November, the day before Walcheren fell, the American 3rd and 7th Armies on the southern sector of the Allied front had crossed the Moselle, while further north the 1st Army toiled forward from Aachen towards the Roer; elsewhere, however, the US 9th and British 2nd Armies in Belgium and Holland were having to fight for every yard of ground, hampered by continual rain and low cloud that prevented the Allied Tactical Air Forces from lending effective support.

For the armies in the north, the great natural barrier that guarded Germany's western frontier – the River Rhine, across which the 1st British Airborne Division had tried and failed to secure a bridgehead at Arnhem the previous September – remained a long way away. November, too, was nearly half over, and it would not be long before the fog and rain gave way to winter snow.

As though to emphasize this fact, a flurry of sleet lashed suddenly against the perspex of the Anson's windscreen. The pilot noted that visibility was growing steadily worse, but it no longer mattered; the Turnhout–Eindhoven road was visible at intervals through the drifting layers of shredded grey cloud and the airfield itself was only five minutes away.

He called up Eindhoven and obtained immediate clearance to land. The sleet intensified as he descended through the stratus, levelling out at a thousand feet over the flat, waterlogged Dutch countryside.

He made a gentle left turn over the village of Veldhoven, bringing the Anson into line with the runway in use. The approach lights, strings of glowing beads beyond the beating windscreen wipers, floated towards him. He came in over the threshold, the Anson's nose at a slight angle to the runway to compensate for a crosswind, then brought it into line once more with a swift touch of rudder as he eased back the stick and closed the throttles in a single, fluid movement. The Anson's mainwheels touched the runway a few moments later, kicking up spray as they passed through large pools of water.

The aircraft's five passengers pressed their faces to the windows as the pilot taxied in, surveying their new home with feelings that varied from excited anticipation to dismay.

Eindhoven bore more than a passing resemblance to a First World War battlefield. There were bomb craters everywhere, filled with water, and the surface of the field was a sea of mud, with not a trace of grass anywhere. Holes in the runways and taxiways and the ground immediately to either side had been hastily filled in and the surface levelled. Months of Allied bombing had wrecked the airfield installations, but the RAF had quickly erected canvas hangars soon after moving into Eindhoven, and flying operations were conducted from caravans and tents.

The dispersals were crammed with aircraft, shrouded under camouflage netting – Typhoons and Tempests mainly, but with a sprinkling of Spitfires and a few Auster army cooperation aircraft. The Anson taxied past the burnt-out wreck of a Junkers 88, which no one had bothered to clear away, and came to a stop a few yards away from a long, low caravan which bore the hastily-painted sign 'Operations'.

The pilot shut down the engines and went back into the fuselage, where his passengers were gathering their kit together, and opened the door, admitting a blast of damp, raw air and a spatter of rain. He picked up a sack of mail and indicated several more which were stacked at the rear of the fuselage.

'Give me a hand with these, chaps, will you?'

Bowed under the weight of their personal kit and the extra burden of the mail, the five replacement pilots squeezed through the exit door and jumped down on to the tarmac, following the Anson pilot towards the caravan. Someone inside opened the door and they filed gratefully through, shaking the rain from themselves. A flying officer, seated at a small trestle table, looked up as they crowded in and addressed the Anson pilot.

'Wotcher, Ken. Stinking weather, as usual.'

'It never varies,' said the Anson pilot, picking up a tin mug from the table, inspecting it closely and tipping the dregs it contained on to the floor of the caravan. 'Any tea on the go?'

'In the urn over there. You blokes' – turning to the replacements – 'you blokes grab some too, I reckon you could do with it. The Boss wants to see you as soon as he gets back. He's out on a sortie at the moment – an absolute glutton for punishment, he is. Everyone else is stood down. Group Control doesn't think there's much to be gained by flying in this weather, but the Boss thinks otherwise. He's gone off with a section of four Tempests to Rheine to try and catch the Huns with their knickers down. Should be due back soon.'

He rummaged around on the table and produced a sheet of paper. 'Let's see,' he muttered. 'Who's who?' He checked off their names, and said: 'That's fine. Two of you for 505 Squadron, two for 473 and one for 449. Hope you don't get yourselves killed, like the last lot did,' he added cheerfully.

The replacement pilots squatted down on the sacks of mail they had just brought in and sipped the hot tea gratefully. The flying officer, pretending to scrutinize some papers, surveyed them covertly; like the Anson pilot, he wondered about the burned man. The others were a pretty routine bunch; one pilot officer and three sergeants, all young, but second-tour men nonetheless. A bit more promising than some of the types the Eindhoven Wing had been getting recently, straight from Operational Training Unit. They hadn't lasted long, and no wonder. They hadn't even been capable of handling the

Tempest properly, never mind fighting the Huns.

A sudden, savage squall of rain hammered the caravan and he cast a worried glance out of the window. Visibility was so bad that he could hardly see the airfield boundary, and the cloud base was getting lower all the time. He hoped the Boss was okay, then smiled inwardly at his fears. The Boss had a sense of direction like a homing pigeon.

Nevertheless, he felt considerable relief when, a minute later, the radio in one corner of the caravan gave a sudden crackle. The set was tuned to the Flying Control frequency, so that the duty officer in Operations could hear what was happening at all times.

'Tramway, Tramway,' a metallic voice said, 'this is Ramrod. Four miles south-east. Requesting immediate pancake.'

The louder tones of Flying Control came back immediately. 'Ramrod, this is Tramway. You are cleared to pancake. Runway in use is zero-nine, surface wind one-one-zero, fifteen knots. Visibility one thousand yards, rain. Queen Fox Easy nine-nine-eight.'

The two pairs of Tempests came straight in to land. The burned man caught sight of them as they slipped in from the east, vague shapes becoming solid outlines as they emerged from the rain-mist. Even on the ground, out of their element, they looked full of power and purpose.

Sydney Camm, chief designer of Hawker Aircraft, the man who had created the legendary Hurricane which had borne the brunt of the fighting in the Battle of Britain, had designed a brilliant fighting machine in the Tempest Mk V. Taking as his basis the Hawker Typhoon fighter-bomber – a big, rugged design which was really a piece of flying artillery – he had turned it into a new aircraft that was the fastest, most potent piston-engined fighter in service anywhere in the world.

From the outset, the Tempest had been designed to achieve air superiority at low and medium levels – in other words, to counter the threat posed by fast enemy fighter-bombers. Its ability to carry 250 gallons of fuel gave it a formidable combat radius of over five hundred miles; operating from bases in the Low Countries it could range as far as Berlin. Its 2,400 horse-power Napier Sabre engine, driving a massive four-bladed de Havilland propeller, gave it an impressive acceleration and a top speed, straight and level, of 440 mph. The aircraft weighed seven tons, and in a dive it could achieve speeds of over 500 mph – a useful margin in an emergency.

The view from the Tempest's cockpit – which was situated well aft, on a level with the trailing edge of the wing – was excellent. The pilot sat under a transparent 'blister'-type cockpit canopy, affording good all-round vision: thanks to the position of the cockpit he could look down and behind, covering the dangerous blind spot which left so many other fighters vulnerable to attack.

At the touch of a thumb, the Tempest pilot could unleash the formidable power of four 20-mm cannon, whose magazines held eight hundred shells – enough for twenty seconds of firing time. Also, like the Typhoon, it could carry two 1,000-lb bombs or eight rocket projectiles, although this configuration was not normally used as it impaired the aircraft's range.

The first Tempest squadrons had been thrown into battle against the V-1 flying bombs, which had been unleashed against southern England in the summer of 1944, and the new fighters had destroyed over six hundred of them. The battle against the 'buzz-bombs', however, had revealed some serious defects in the Tempest's Sabre engine, and at the end of September the aircraft had been temporarily withdrawn from service while the snags were ironed out.

A month later, two Tempest squadrons – Nos 505 and 473 – had been sent to Eindhoven as part of the 2nd Tactical Air Force. They were accompanied by a third squadron, No. 449, flying Spitfire XIVs.

Together, they made a formidable team. No. 505 Squadron had been in the thick of the fighting right from the start; an Auxiliary Air Force unit, it had fought in France in the dark days of 1940 as part of the RAF's Advanced Air Striking Force, and in the months that followed the evacuation from Dunkirk its pilots had chalked up an impressive score of enemy aircraft destroyed during the Battle of Britain. After that, flying Spitfires, it had taken part in offensive fighter operations over Occupied Europe for three years, on and off, and in 1944 it had been one of the first RAF squadrons to cross over to France in the wake of the Allied invasion.

The second squadron of the Eindhoven Wing, No. 473, was a Royal Australian Air Force unit and, flying Curtiss Kittyhawks and later Spitfires, had fought in North Africa and Sicily before coming to England to join other Spitfire squadrons in carrying out fighter 'sweeps' over France and the Low Countries. Following closely on the heels of No. 505, the Australians had crossed the Channel and begun operations from Normandy shortly after D-Day.

The Eindhoven Wing's third unit, No. 449 (Royal Canadian Air Force) Squadron, had been formed in the summer of 1942 and had begun its career as a fighter-bomber squadron. Equipped with bomb-carrying Hurricane IIs, it had spent the first few months of its existence carrying out hazardous low-level attacks on 'pinpoint' targets such as radar stations on the coasts of France and Belgium, and had suffered very heavy losses in the process. Re-equipping with Spitfire 9s in 1943, it had received the much more powerful Mk XIVs the following year and had taken part in the battle against the flying-bombs. When Nos 505 and 473 Squadrons had returned to England to re-equip with Tempests in September, No. 449 had joined them and gone to Holland with them, still flying its Spitfires. Its primary task now was to provide top cover for the Tempests.

Through the rain-streaked windows of the caravan, the burned man watched the four Tempests as they taxied in, weaving from side to side as their pilots strove to see past the long engine cowlings. They swung on to their dispersals, the pilots using rudder and short bursts of throttle to turn their noses into wind. One by one, the whirling propellers became motionless and the rumble of the engines died away.

The burned man looked with interest at the nearer Tempest, its outline blurred by the rivulets of rain. What might have been a smile puckered the scars around his mouth as he watched the cockpit canopy slide back and the pilot emerge, feeling with his toes for the little hollows, covered with sprung hinges, that were built into the side of the Tempest's fuselage above the wing. Standing on the latter, the pilot reached up and closed the canopy to keep out the rain, then he jumped down and ran towards the operations caravan, head lowered against the heavy drops.

He burst into the caravan and slammed the door shut behind him, shaking himself like a dog and showering the other occupants with water. Throwing his flying-helmet and oxygen mask on to the table he made straight for the tea urn and poured himself a mugful, taking a long swallow and surveying the newcomers over the rim.

His eyes met those of the burned man, and his left eyelid drooped in a barely perceptible wink. Then he set down his empty mug, shrugged off his flying-jacket and threw it into a corner. Now, for the first time, the newcomers saw the Wing Commander's rank braid on the epaulettes of his battledress, and the ribbons underneath his pilot's wings: the DSO, the DFC and Bar, and the DFM.

Suddenly, the Wing Commander gave a broad grin. 'Welcome to Eindhoven,' he said. 'My name's Yeoman.' He pointed a thumb towards a second bedraggled figure that entered the caravan, dripping water. 'And this is Squadron Leader Tim Phelan, OC 505 Squadron.'

'Hiya,' Phelan said, giving the new pilots a cursory glance. Like Yeoman, he made a beeline for the tea urn. 'Carter and Dawlish have gone off to Flying Control,' he said, naming the other two pilots who had just returned from the recent sortie. 'One of their pals over there is going into Eindhoven and they've organized a lift.'

'That reminds me,' Yeoman said, turning to the seated flying officer, 'can we get hold of some transport for these chaps? My car is picking me up in a few minutes' time, but apart from Squadron Leader Phelan there's only room for one more passenger, so I'll take the flight lieutenant, here.' He nodded at the burned man.

'Right, sir,' the flying officer said, reaching for a telephone. Yeoman perched himself on the edge of the trestle table and looked at the new pilots, smiling.

'I don't suppose your first impression of Eindhoven is very favourable,' he said. 'However, there is one crumb of comfort

– we are all billeted in the town itself, and the Dutch have made things quite cosy for us.'

He stuck a hand in his battledress pocket, pulled out a battered briar pipe, inspected it closely to make sure that there was still some tobacco in it, and lit it. A cloud of evil-smelling smoke drifted through the caravan, and one of the new sergeant pilots politely stifled a cough.

Yeoman chatted away for a few more minutes, contentedly smoking his pipe. He never once mentioned anything remotely connected with operational flying, and the burned man knew that this was deliberate; the Wing Commander was setting out to make the new arrivals feel completely at ease, while appraising them at the same time. There would be plenty of opportunity to present the hard facts to them in the morning.

There was the sound of a motor outside. Yeoman got up and rubbed a clear patch on one of the windows, which had misted over.

'All right, lads,' he said, 'there's your taxi. You'll find some food laid on for you in Eindhoven. I'll see you for a beer later on this evening, maybe, but in any case I want you to come to my office – the hut next to 505 Squadron Dispersal – at 0800 tomorrow. Bring your log-books with you and don't miss the bus from Eindhoven, it's a bloody long walk.'

He turned to the Anson pilot, who had been half dozing on top of his pile of mail bags.

'I expect you'll be staying the night too, Ken?' he asked.

The Anson pilot nodded, rising to his feet. 'Too true, sir.' He pointed at the leaden sky. 'No chance of churning my way through that lot – I value my little pink body far too much.'

'You'd better get on the truck, then,' Yeoman told him. 'You might have to bunk up with somebody, though; accommodation is pretty full at the moment, because there's a Typhoon Wing here in addition to ourselves.'

'We'll draw lots for him,' Tim Phelan grinned.

The Anson pilot tapped the side of his nose significantly. 'Don't worry,' he said, 'I have my connections in Eindhoven. A widow, she is, and very nice too. I keep my spare toothbrush there.' He followed the others out of the caravan.

Yeoman swung round suddenly to face the burned man and a broad grin split his features. In two strides he was across the caravan, clasping the burned man's scarred hand warmly.

'Simon! You old so-and-so – it's damned good to see you!'

The burned man's face twisted. 'You too, George,' he said quietly. 'It's been a long time. I thought for a moment you hadn't recognized me – although I wouldn't blame you for that.' There was no trace of bitterness in the burned man's voice.

'Oh, I'm sorry about that, Simon,' Yeoman said mildly. 'I just thought it might have been a bit unnerving for the other replacements to discover that one of their number was an old pal of mine.'

He turned to Tim Phelan, who had been listening to the exchange with interest. 'Tim, I'd like you to meet Simon Wynne-Williams. We flew with 505 Squadron as NCO pilots in France in 1940, and in the Battle of Britain. That is, until –'

He broke off, embarrassed, and Wynne-Williams finished the sentence for him.

'Until I stopped a 109's cannon shell in my petrol tank, the result of which encounter you see here.' He pointed to his ravaged face. 'Actually, it might have been a lot worse – the medics didn't do a bad job in patching me up. In fact, the skin of my face is made up mainly of grafts from my backside. So if anyone kisses me these days, I take great delight in telling them that they've just kissed my arse.'

They laughed, the tension broken. Wynne-Williams' voice gave no indication of the two and a half years of agony he had suffered in the Burns Unit at East Grinstead, while dedicated plastic surgeons painstakingly rebuilt his face and hands. Philosophically, he believed that he had been far luckier than most; in the same ward there had been a bomber navigator with no eyes, and another pilot whose hands and forearms had been burned completely away below the elbows. At least he, Wynne-Williams, had been discharged with all his faculties, permitting him to return to operational flying. That was the important thing; the fact that his once-handsome features no longer existed had ceased to trouble him now he was back in action.

The road to Eindhoven was potholed and waterlogged. Despite hurried repairs, carried out with the help of locally-recruited labour, it still bore the scars inflicted over the past months by Allied fighter-bombers as they harried the retreating Wehrmacht. Yeoman's car – a Mercedes which had been found abandoned in a ditch on the airfield perimeter and which had presumably once been the property of a Luftwaffe officer – lurched violently as the driver spun the wheel this way and that in a bid to avoid the worst of the ruts; a hopeless task, for the road surface had been churned up even more in recent weeks by the passage of countless tracked vehicles. This afternoon, for a change, there was no movement on the road. Once, they passed a column of a dozen Sherman tanks, parked in the mud by the roadside; as they passed the leading tank a few soldiers, huddled under drenched capes, peered miserably at them through the rain. Apart from that dismal group, there was no sign of life.

Eindhoven was a grey town, filled with grey people. It had not always been so. At the turn of the century, Eindhoven had been a typical, thriving rural community of some six thousand people, the majority of whom had never strayed further than neighbouring villages. The great industrialist Anton Philips had altered all that. By the late 1930s, his new electrical components factories had transformed Eindhoven into a huge industrial town, one of the best-equipped and most modern centres of production in the world. In 1940, it had been one of the richest prizes to fall into the hands of the invading Germans, who had not been slow to turn its resources over to their wartime needs.

Sadly, the German possession of the Philips factories had turned Eindhoven into a primary Allied target. Time after time during the four bitter years that followed the enemy occupation the factories had been hit by the bombers of the RAF and, later, the USAAF. In an attempt to spare Dutch lives, and for the sake of precision, these attacks had been carried out at low level and in daylight, but despite the gallant efforts of the Allied aircrews – who had suffered heavy losses in the process – the town itself had inevitably sustained severe damage. The war had dropped a grey veil over Eindhoven.

One day, it would be lifted. In the meantime, now that the Allies were here, the inhabitants were content to bear their privations and wait for the better things to come.

Dusk was falling as the Mercedes entered the outskirts of the town, bumping over slippery cobbled streets that were crammed with military vehicles of all kinds. The driver turned into a square, surrounded by trees on three sides. On the remaining side, a big gateway flanked by stone pillars and a high wall gave access to a forecourt and a grey, featureless building whose rows of small windows and plain wooden door spoke of austerity.

The car drew up and the occupants got out, shivering in the cold, moist air. Yeoman smiled in the gloom.

'Well, Simon, this is home – for the time being, at least. You are about to sleep in a convent.'

'Are any of the nuns still around?' Wynne-Williams wanted to know.

'Oh, no. They left a long time ago, shortly after the Germans came. The last occupants were the Waffen SS. At least they left the place tidy, which is more than it is now. Come on, let's get out of this damned rain.'

They went inside, pushing their way past a dusty blackout curtain, and found themselves at the end of a long corridor. Doors on either side opened on to small rooms that were filled with camp beds, kitbags, flying clothing and other items of pilots' equipment. Bodies, in various stages of undress, were sprawled on a few of the beds, but most were empty. The whole place stank of sweat, wet clothing, beer and fried bacon.

'It's a bit less unsavoury upstairs,' Yeoman told him. 'That's where the flight lieutenants and above live. Apart from our own batmen – we share one between four of us, by the way – we employ a couple of old Dutchmen to come along and muck us out twice a week. Come on.'

He led the way up a narrow, winding staircase to the floor above. Here, too, small cell-like rooms, each containing two beds, opened on to another long corridor. Phelan disappeared into one of the rooms, while Yeoman conducted Wynne-Williams to another some way down the corridor. The door was open, and the room was empty.

'There you are, Simon,' Yeoman said. 'You'll be sharing with Jackie Burgess; he's on leave at the moment.'

Wynne-Williams peered inside the room, reached round the door jamb and switched on the light. One of the beds inside was cluttered with odds and ends; the other was empty except for a few blankets, stacked in a neat pile. A few pin-ups graced the walls, which were otherwise barren apart from a battered crucifix. Wynne-Williams noticed that Christ had lost his head, and that the wall around the crucifix was pock-marked with bullet holes.

'The work of the Waffen SS?' he queried.

'The work of Dick Coombes,' Yeoman corrected him. 'He was the previous occupant of your bed. He woke up one night and started blazing away at old J.C. with his revolver – scared the shits out of all of us. He swore blind that Jesus was coming down to get him. He might have been right, at that, because he got the chop a couple of days later.'

'Charming,' Wynne-Williams commented wryly. He gave the remains of the crucifix a mock salute and sat down on the edge of his bed, looking up at Yeoman quizzically.

'I suppose I ought to call you "sir", in view of your present exalted position,' he said.

'Yes, I suppose you ought to,' the other replied, smiling. 'It just doesn't seem right, somehow, though. I owe you a lot, Simon, and I often think about those early days in France. God, it seems a long time ago.'

There was a semi-embarrassed pause, then Yeoman said: 'Anyway, we'll have a good old yarn over a beer before dinner, and I'll fill you in about the operational side of things here.' He glanced at his watch. 'Dinner is at seven, and unless we're on duty we always change into number one uniform. See you in the bar at six-thirty? If you take the stairs at the opposite end of the corridor, you'll find the bar on the left-hand side at the bottom.'

Yeoman smiled and went out, closing the door behind him. Wynne-Williams listened to his footfalls receding along the corridor, shrugged and smiled to himself, as though enjoying some secret joke. Then he threw his kitbag into a corner, pushed the mound of blankets aside and stretched out on the bed, his hands clasped behind his head. After a while, despite the chill in the room, he dozed off.

He awoke, drenched in perspiration, to blind, unreasoning panic. Wildly he looked about him, not remembering where he was. The last vestiges of daylight had long since gone and the cold darkness closed in on him, beating his face with its wings. The only sound in the room was the incessant spatter of the rain against the panes of the solitary tiny window, and it was this reassuring, everyday noise that brought him slowly back to reality.

He sat up and swung his legs over the edge of the bed, leaning forward with his elbows on his knees, his face buried in his hands. He was trembling violently, but he knew that it would pass. The sweat began to dry on his body and he shivered. Groping in the darkness, he found a blanket and draped it over his shoulders, pulling it round his body like a cloak. It was slightly damp, but it helped to keep the cold at bay.

The dream was always the same. It was not like earlier dreams, in which all-consuming flames had reduced him to screaming, mindless insensibility; in a way, the new dream was infinitely more terrifying, a dream of cold, clammy darkness that whispered in the deepest recesses of his mind for days afterwards.

Feeling slightly sick, he took a deep breath and looked at the luminous dial of his watch. It was 0615. He rose and, groping his way in the blackness, crossed over to the doorway and felt for the light switch. A moment later he stood blinking in the sudden harsh glare of a naked electric light bulb, surveying his surroundings clearly for the first time.

He went over and quickly closed the shutters at the little window, blocking out the rain-swept night. The simple action had the effect of steadying his nerves a little; he held out his hands in front of him and studied them intently, seeing the tremors subside little by little until finally the hands were still.

Satisfied, he picked up his kitbag and emptied its contents on to the bed. Retrieving his best uniform from the pile, he draped it over a hanger, smoothing out the creases, and hung it from a nail behind the door. Turning away, he automatically felt his chin for stubble, then smiled to himself; the last time he had shaved had been in September 1940, before the searing flames of high-octane petrol burned away the skin of his face.

A sudden sharp rap on the door startled him and he swung round, reaching for the handle, but the door opened before his hand made contact and a small, tubby airman burst into the room, carrying an enamel bowl and a steaming bucket. Ignoring Wynne-Williams completely, he set down the bowl with a clatter on the small locker beside the latter's bed and tipped a careful measure of the bucket's contents into the receptacle. Only then did he speak, addressing the pilot in an almost unintelligible accent which, Wynne-Williams guessed, had its origins in the slums of Glasgow.

'Guidevenin' sorr. Ah thochtye'd likeadrap o'hotwatter. Ah'm McGann. Ah'll seet'ye.'

The man grinned lopsidedly and bundled himself out of the room, leaving the pilot standing in open-mouthed amazement. Once again Wynne-Williams began to shake all over. Sitting down heavily on the edge of his bed, he burst into an uncontrollable fit of laughter. The tears coursed down his cheeks, washing away the awful tension he had experienced only minutes before.

After a little while, still chuckling, he got up and washed carefully in the hot water the extraordinary McGann had brought him. There was a new briskness in his movements as he changed into his other uniform, and a few minutes later, as he made his way down the stairs towards the bar, he realized with some surprise that he was whistling a little tune. It was as though, somehow, the clock had been turned back four years.

He opened the door of the bar and stood there for a moment, peering through the haze of tobacco smoke at the press of blue uniforms, listening to the hubbub of voices. In a corner of the bar Yeoman was standing with arm upraised, beckoning to him.

His dark dream forgotten, Wynne-Williams pushed his way through the throng. He was happy now, for he knew that this was where he belonged. Once again, he was part of an operational squadron.

2

Oberstleutnant Joachim Richter stared at the sheet of paper he had just lifted from the pile that lay on his desk top and frowned deeply. After studying the document for a few moments, he pressed a buzzer. Almost instantly, a door flew open and a young, blond lieutenant entered the office, clicking his heels sharply and stiffening like a ramrod to the position of attention. Richter looked at the earnest face and the immaculately pressed uniform with vague annoyance; his adjutant, Hasso von Gleiwitz, always made him feel slightly uncomfortable. The man – the son of an aristocratic Prussian family with a military pedigree as long as one's arm – was a conceited prig, and by no means popular with his fellow officers. He was also unswervingly loyal to whoever was his immediate superior, and for the last few months that superior had been Richter. Not only that; the man was a damned fine adjutant, with an uncanny perception for small detail in whatever job he tackled, and an ice-cold incisive voice which, on occasion, had been known to send shivers up the spines of officers several times his senior.

'Hasso,' Richter said, waving the sheet of paper, 'just what the hell is all this about?'

The lieutenant inclined the top half of his body slightly, leaning forward to get a better view of the document, then straightened himself again.

'Orders from the Oberkommando der Luftwaffe, sir, asking for lists of personnel surplus to our immediate requirements. For transfer to the Eastern Front as temporary infantrymen, sir.'

'Infantry!' Richter roared in sudden fury. 'Surplus personnel! What do those fat-arsed, chairbound bastards in the OKL think we are!'

Von Gleiwitz winced almost imperceptibly. Privately, he thought that his outspoken commanding officer would get himself into trouble one day, if he happened to air his views when the wrong people were listening. Yet he knew that Richter was right; serious though the situation in the east might be, the Luftwaffe needed every single man to keep its fighter squadrons operational.

Richter took a deep breath and calmed down a little. He stared hard at the lieutenant, then tapped the paper and said in a low, even voice:

'Hasso, I have not seen this. Have you?'

Von Gleiwitz looked straight ahead, his eyes fixed on a photograph of a Focke-Wulf 190 that hung on the far wall. 'No, sir,' he said woodenly.

Richter screwed the offending document into a ball and tossed it into the waste-paper basket with studied contempt.

'Will that be all, sir?' von Gleiwitz asked. Richter nodded.

'Yes, thank you, Hasso,' he said tiredly. 'No – wait a minute. Tell someone to get a pot of coffee going and give Major Schumacher a ring. I'd like him to join me.'

Von Gleiwitz clicked his heels again and went out. Richter pushed back his chair, got up and crossed over to the window, staring moodily at the lowering rain-clouds. The downpour which had drenched northern Europe for several days now continued unabated, although according to the weather boys the clouds would start to break up in the course of the afternoon. Nevertheless, this grey, wet morning of Monday, 13 November, was just about as depressing as any Richter had known.

He took a case from his pocket and extracted a long cigar, rolling it thoughtfully between his fingers as he stared out over the rain-swept surface of Rheine airfield. It was deserted, for the aircraft that were not undergoing maintenance in the hangars were dispersed in carefully concealed blast-proof shelters around the perimeter.

Richter lit his cigar and turned away from the rain-streaked window, resting his weight lightly on the sill. His eyes roved over the photographs on the wall behind his desk, every one of which told a story. France, 1940; Russia 1941; Sicily, the following year, when the Luftwaffe had made an abortive attempt to smash Malta. . . . He looked at the young, eager, smiling faces with infinite sadness, and the boys who had been his companions looked back at him as they clustered in front of their Messerschmitts and Focke-Wulfs. Most of them were gone now, the ashes of their bodies scattered over the battlegrounds of Europe, the Balkans and the Middle East.

Those that were left, like himself, had the almost impossible task of welding the stream of replacement pilots into an efficient fighting force capable of taking on the ever-growing hordes of Allied fighters and bombers that now swarmed across the Third Reich. There was no doubt that the new pilots were keen enough to play their part in the defence of Germany, but there was no time to train them properly, and unless they were very lucky they soon fell victim to experienced Allied fighter leaders or to their own inexperience, which resulted in an appalling accident rate. The sad truth was that as 1944 drew to a close, the Luftwaffe was producing fighter aircraft in greater numbers than ever before – but the new generation of German pilots was lacking in the necessary skill and experience to get the best out of these machines.

Richter's thoughts turned wistfully to the Luftwaffe's new jet fighter, the Messerschmitt 262. Faster than any Allied fighter by a good hundred miles an hour, formidably armed with four 30-mm cannon, it could have swept the British and Americans from the skies in the summer of 1944 if it had been available in sufficient numbers – but Hitler had become obsessed with the idea of turning this superlative aircraft into a 'reprisal bomber', and had ordered that all Me 262s coming off the production line should be fitted with bomb racks. This, together with the disruption caused by the Allied bombing offensive, had set the whole Me 262 programme back by at least six months, and only now were a few of the jets beginning to reach the fighter squadrons.

There were twenty-five Me 262 jet fighter-bombers at Rheine, together with a mixed collection of 120 other fighters

– Messerschmitt 109s, Focke-Wulf 190s, and a few Junkers 188s, the latter earmarked for night defence. Together, they formed the complement of Jagdgeschwader 66, the fighter wing which Joachim Richter commanded.

The badge of Jagdgeschwader 66, a leaping panther, formed the centrepiece of the collection of photographs on the office wall. The good old 66th, thought Richter. It was almost five years since he had joined the Wing as a raw and untried pilot at the beginning of 1940, before the hectic days of the offensive in France and Flanders, and he had served on and off with it ever since, apart from one or two special assignments and a tour of duty with an experimental fighter unit.

Now he had returned as commanding officer, transformed in less than five short years from a fledgling into a full-blown fighter ace with eighty-five victories to his credit, five more than the legendary von Richthofen had scored in the First World War. Most of those victories had been achieved on the Russian Front, in the early days when the Soviet Air Force was reeling in chaos before the German onslaught; the successes had been fewer after the middle of 1943, on both east and west fronts.

Richter knew with absolute certainty now that the war was lost, as did so many of his comrades. Some of them, a few months earlier, had taken drastic action and attempted to assassinate Hitler; they had failed, and most of them had ended up dangling from meat hooks in concentration camps. Richter shuddered to think how narrowly he had missed being implicated in the Bomb Plot, as the affair had come to be known. An approach had once been made to him in tentative fashion, at a party, by an army colonel who had eventually questioned him about his loyalty to Germany, rather than to the Führer; but Richter had refused to make any revealing remarks or to commit himself to anything. He trusted no one, for in wartime Germany that was the recipe for survival. Nevertheless, in the days following the attempt on Hitler's life he had lived in a state of constant anxiety, half expecting a visit from the Gestapo or the Field Security Police, not knowing whether his name might have been on a list of possible anti-Hitler sympathizers drawn up by the conspirators and subsequently seized by the authorities. Obviously it had not been, or he would not now still be here.

He went back to his desk and, with a sigh of resignation, continued working his way through the stack of paperwork. Most of it simply required his signature, but he never signed anything without reading it first; he had known of more than one commander who had got into serious trouble by failing to pay enough attention to what appeared in his in tray.

He had been busy at his task for fifteen minutes when von Gleiwitz appeared and announced the arrival of Major Schumacher. The latter came in and saluted; the adjutant relieved him of his dripping overcoat and went back into the outer office.

'Come in, Johnny,' Richter said warmly. 'Come in and sit down. There'll be some coffee along in a minute. Sorry to drag you over here in the rain; I just felt the need of a chat and the sight of your ugly mug.'

The commanding officer of No. 1 Squadron, Jagdgeschwader 66 – and Richter's second in command of the Wing – looked glum. Without being asked, he took a cigarette from the box on Richter's desk. There was no formality between the two men; they had been close friends for too long, and shared too many dangers. 'Have you heard the news?' he asked suddenly.

Richter looked at him questioningly. 'No. What news?'

'The Tommies have sunk the *Tirpitz*.'

'Good God! When?' Richter knew that the great battleship, the pride of the German Navy, had been lying at anchor in a Norwegian fjord for many months, surrounded by an array of anti-torpedo nets and anti-aircraft guns. The British had attacked her on several occasions, using both aircraft and midget submarines, but had only succeeded in damaging the 43,000-ton giant. Now it seemed that they had finished her at last, and it did not seem possible.

'It happened sometime yesterday,' Schumacher answered. 'The details haven't been generally released yet, but I've just come from Bruckner's office' – he named Rheine's Senior Intelligence Officer – 'and he showed me a copy of a report that's just come over the teletype, circulated to all fighter commands by the Fliegerführer Kirkenes, in Norway. It seems that the battleship was attacked by a force of Lancasters, using very large bombs, and they made short work of her. The bombers got clean away, too; there wasn't one of our fighters in the air. There'll no doubt be the usual spate of excuses and recriminations,' the Major concluded wryly.

One more nail in Germany's coffin, Richter thought. Defeat in both west and east, defeat in the air, defeat at sea. He felt old and weary, knowing that all the sacrifices of the past five years had been in vain. Nothing but a miracle could save Germany now.

An orderly came in with the coffee, poured out two cups and left. Richter took a tentative sip and made a face.

'God, that's awful,' he said. 'What I'd give for a cup of real coffee again, instead of this ersatz!'

Schumacher raised an eyebrow. 'You can get it,' he commented, 'if you move in the right circles, just like anything else. Do you remember that party we went to in Berlin, last August?'

Richter remembered it very well. Both men had had a few days' leave due to them, and since Schumacher had relatives in Berlin they had decided to spend it there. One evening, as they had been getting pleasantly drunk in a night club reserved for officers, someone – Richter couldn't remember who – had invited them to a party at a house in one of Berlin's exclusive suburbs, so far unscarred by Allied bombing.

Their anticipation had quickly turned to disgust. In a Germany where the majority of the population was existing on rations hardly fit for pigs, the guests at this party had been guzzling every imaginable kind of drink, gorging themselves on beef, ham, roast pork and fowl, and delicacies no doubt looted and hoarded from the occupied territories. And the guests themselves . . . Richter's mouth still twisted in distaste when he thought of them. Haughty women, glittering with diamonds, willing to sell their aristocratic bodies to the highest bidder; senior officers of the SS and the SD and the various political branches of the Nazi Party, boasting of their conquests and, as the drink took hold of them, of the atrocities they had committed in the name of the Third Reich.

And there had been the much decorated Paratroop colonel, his left arm missing, who had emerged from the shadows like a spectre and, before anyone could intervene, had overturned one of the groaning tables, shattering dozens of bottles and spattering their contents over immaculate uniforms and costly dresses. Richter could still see the puffy, outraged faces that had gaped at him open-mouthed, hear the gasps and stifled screams of the women and the crunch of splintered glass as the colonel strode stiff-backed through the débris towards the door, spitting out a single word:

'Bastards!'

They, too, had made their exit then, knowing that they had just witnessed the end of a man's career, and perhaps even of his life – hating themselves inwardly, too, because they had not had the courage to do what he had done.

The memory of that party – and, indeed, of Berlin itself, with its unhealthy mixture of misery and forced gaiety – depressed him. It was time to change the subject. He picked up a green folder from his desk and passed it to Schumacher.

'I'd like you to take a look at that, Johnny. It's the dossier our Intelligence boys have compiled on the new RAF fighter wing that moved into Eindhoven a month or so ago – the one whose Tempests have been giving us a little bit of bother.'

Schumacher opened the folder and began to read through the contents in silence, sipping his coffee from time to time. After a while, he put the folder aside and gazed at Richter thoughtfully.

'Quite an experienced outfit, by the look of things,' he commented. 'And the commanding officer – what's his name? Ah yes, Yeoman. He's not exactly a novice, either, is he?'

Richter corrected Schumacher's pronunciation of Yeoman's name and said:

'No, he isn't. Quite a hot cookie, by all accounts. Thirty victories to his credit or thereabouts, which is pretty high for an RAF pilot. Don't forget, the RAF didn't have the benefit of the turkey-shoot we enjoyed on the Russian Front. It's strange, but in many ways his career seems to have run parallel to my own. France, then the Battle of Britain, as the Tommies call it, then North Africa and Malta. He apparently commanded a Mosquito squadron before his present job.'

'Why the interest in this particular unit?' Schumacher wanted to know. 'The Tempest is the best fighter the Allies have got, admittedly, but I can't see them being too much of a threat to us here. They won't risk our flak.'

In this he was right; Rheine was the most heavily-defended airfield in Germany, with long lanes of quadruple 20-mm anti-aircraft guns protecting the approaches to the main runway and many more gun positions scattered around the airfield perimeter. Together, they were capable of putting up a veritable steel umbrella over the head of any aircraft that was landing or taking off – an umbrella which, most Allied fighter pilots had already decided, was sheer suicide to try and penetrate.

'You miss the point, Johnny,' Richter said reprovingly. 'Very soon, we shall have a considerable force of Messerschmitt 262 jets here at Rheine, all of them committed to attacking the Allied forces across the Rhine. They will be capable of inflicting considerable damage, so you can bet that the Allies will do everything in their power to knock them out. Now, since they won't risk attacking them here, on the airfield, they'll try and catch them on the way home, when the jets are short of fuel – and you can also bet that they'll use the Tempests to do the job. Don't forget that the Tempest is the only Allied fighter with a reasonable chance of catching a 262, especially at low level.'

'So we're going to have to beat the Tommies at their own game?' Schumacher queried. Richter nodded.

'That's right. We're going to have to keep them on their toes all the time by maintaining regular patrols over the approach to Eindhoven whenever a 262 sortie goes out. It'll mean some very close liaison work with the jet boys, and it will be risky, for we shall be operating at medium and low level and are likely to meet a lot of opposition from the enemy flak. I can't see any other way of dealing with the problem, though.'

He stared thoughtfully at the green folder for a few moments, then said:

'I wonder what this Yeoman fellow is thinking right at this very moment? I wish I could meet him.'

'Perhaps you will, and sooner than you think,' Schumacher smiled. 'If things continue to go on the way they are, he'll probably be sitting in your chair before very long!'

Richter laughed. 'I don't give a damn who sits in this chair, Johnny, so long as he doesn't have a red star on his hat. I don't think it will come to that, though; I still believe that we can hold the Allies on the Rhine until they come to their senses and agree to the armistice terms we are bound to put forward, sooner or later. It's the only way out for us now, Johnny.'

'So you don't reckon much to all this talk about new secret weapons which will supposedly soon win the war for us?' Schumacher asked.

'No, I don't. We can't win the war now, Johnny; that's an impossibility. There's too much stacked against us. But we can force the Western Allies and the Reds into a situation where they'll forget all about this unconditional surrender nonsense and agree to armistice talks. We can do it by gaining total air superiority over the territory of the Reich.'

He leaned forward over the desk, emphasizing his words with short stabs of his index finger. 'We need fighters, Johnny. Fighters and still more fighters. Aircraft like the Messerschmitt 262, in their hundreds, so that we can smash the Allied bomber formations and give our war industries some respite. Then we'll show the Allies that Germany is not finished yet! We'll make them realize that an invasion of our Fatherland will be such a costly undertaking that they'll never dare attempt it.'

'But the Führer will never sue for an armistice,' Schumacher objected.

Richter gazed at him steadily. His companion met his eyes and nodded slowly in answer to the message that was best left unspoken. The problem of Adolf Hitler was one that could still be resolved by the German armed forces, when the time was right. . . .

The commander of Jagdgeschwader 66 got up suddenly and strode over to the window, rubbing one of the panes with the palm of his hand to clear away the condensation. The rain had stopped, and there seemed to be brighter patches among the grey cloud masses.

Richter returned to his desk and reached for the telephone. A minute later he replaced the receiver, a broad smile on his face.

'The weather's starting to break up nicely, Johnny,' he told Schumacher. 'Let's get over to Operations. I think we might just pop across the Rhine and tickle up the Tommies this afternoon.'

The Focke-Wulf 190D-9 fighter was a vastly more potent fighting machine than the earlier FW 190A models with which, two years earlier, the Luftwaffe had for a time wrested air superiority from the RAF's Spitfire squadrons over France. Fitted with a Jumo 213 radial engine that could be boosted to 2,240 horsepower by means of water-methanol injection, the 'Dora-Nine', as it was known to its pilots, could reach a speed of 440 mph at 37,000 feet. It was armed with two 20-mm MG 151 cannon and two 13-mm MG 131 machine-guns.

Because of the new engine, the nose of the Dora-Nine was much longer than that of the earlier FW 190 models, which made taxi-ing a difficult and painfully slow business. This was a constant source of worry to Richter; with the German fighter airfields under continual threat of attack, it was risky to spend too long on their exposed surfaces. Now, as he led the line of twelve Focke-Wulfs out to their take-off position at the end of Rheine's long runway, moving the long nose from side to side with use of the rudder and careful bursts of power so that he could see the way ahead, he kept craning his neck to scan the clouds above and behind. It would be just like the Tommies, he thought, to pop down out of the overcast with a section of Tempests, shoot up the field and make their escape before the anti-aircraft gunners had time to react.

But the sky remained empty and the Focke-Wulfs reached the runway without hindrance, lining up on it in pairs. Over to the right, Richter could see several Me 262s parked by the side of a long wood that concealed their blast shelters. Clouds of steam rose behind them as the hot gases from their turbojets seared the sodden ground.

Richter glanced to his left, where Schumacher's aircraft was positioned alongside, and saw the Major wave briefly, indicating that he was ready to go. Richter acknowledged, then released the brakes and opened the throttle slowly, ruddering to keep straight as the Focke-Wulf started to move. A slight forward pressure on the stick brought the tail up and a few seconds later he was airborne, raising the undercarriage and starting a gentle turn to the left, over the airfield buildings.

The twelve Focke-Wulfs levelled out at three thousand feet, just under the cloud base, and set course to 240 degrees. Behind them, at Rheine, the Messerschmitt 262s were taxi-ing out for take-off.

The operational plan called for six bomb-carrying jets to attack armoured convoys between Maastricht and Aachen. The Focke-Wulfs, in the meantime, would sweep the area to the south of Eindhoven, looking for any RAF fighters that might be alerted to cut off the jets' escape route. The jets had further to go, but their higher speed meant that they would be starting their attack just as the piston-engined fighters entered their patrol area.

The flat landscape of northern Germany slipped quickly by under the Focke-Wulfs' wings as they sped on, their cockpit canopies almost brushing the swirling grey vapour of the cloud base. They skimmed the southern outskirts of Bocholt and a couple of minutes later they were streaking over the broad ribbon of the Rhine. Fifteen miles further on was the River Maas, and beyond that enemy territory.

Their entry into the latter was signalled by a stream of glowing anti-aircraft shells that came up at them from the corner of a wood, briefly lighting up the leaden sky. The fire was wide of the mark and the Focke-Wulfs flew on, ignoring it, their pilots searching the narrow corridor between the clouds and the earth for any sign of enemy fighters.

They crossed the parallel waterways of the Deurne and Bois le Duc Canals, and a minute later picked up the railway line that ran southwards from Eindhoven and then curved away eastwards in the direction of Roermond. Richter decided to take his fighters a few miles farther west, as far as Valkenswaard, and then sweep back towards the railway line, across the track of any enemy aircraft that might be heading south from Eindhoven. As additional insurance, he ordered half his formation to climb up through the clouds and circle just over the tops; he could call them down if he needed them, and they would give warning of any Allied fighters that might be approaching from high altitude.

With Richter leading, the six remaining Focke-Wulfs passed Valkenswaard village at two thousand feet and swung round in a 180-degree turn to the right to head back in the opposite direction. As he rolled back into level flight, Richter caught sight of an aircraft about two miles to the north, flying south-west at low level. In this vicinity, a lone aircraft could only be an enemy. Quickly, he alerted the rest of his pilots and they sped towards it.

Flight Lieutenant Ken Slater, the pilot of the duty Anson, had taken off from Eindhoven only minutes earlier, taking advantage of the first real break in the weather for twenty-four hours or more. It was his misfortune that the light wind was from the east; taking off in that direction, he brought the Anson round in a right-handed turn over Veldhoven, south of the airfield, intending to follow the main road that led through Turnhout to Antwerp. It was at that moment that the enemy pilots sighted him; if he had taken off towards the west he would have escaped undetected.

He had just picked up the road, and was settling down on course, when Eindhoven control warned him urgently that enemy fighters were in the vicinity. Immediately, he opened the throttles and took the Anson up towards the shelter of the clouds, frantically searching the sky as he did so.

He was too late: the Focke-Wulfs were almost upon him. There was no time to shout a warning to the occupants of the Anson's draughty cabin – two pilots whose operational tours were over and who were flying back to England for a well-earned rest. Their first inkling that something was wrong came when Slater threw the Anson into a tight turn, pulling round hard towards the enemy fighters.

Slater's sudden manoeuvre took Joachim Richter completely by surprise. He opened fire from the beam, anticipating a relatively easy deflection shot, but as the British pilot turned steeply his tracers went well to the left of their target and spattered themselves harmlessly over the Dutch countryside.

The two tour-expired pilots in the rear of the Anson clung to their seats, white-faced and gasping with fear, as Slater twisted away from the shells, desperately striving to gain height with each new turn.

It was a hopeless, forlorn effort; there were too many enemy fighters playing cat-and-mouse with him, cutting across his turns. Warrant Officer Weiss, Richter's wingman, throttled back to match the Anson's speed and saw his cannon shells punch into the British aircraft's port wing just inboard of the engine. Instantly, white petrol vapour streamed back in the slipstream; the Anson faltered out of its turn and started to go down in a shallow dive, its nose creeping round in the direction of Eindhoven.

Slater knew now that his only chance was to try and bring the damaged aircraft back within range of Eindhoven's anti-aircraft defences. Weaving from side to side, he dropped to hedge-top height.

Behind him, someone screamed in pain as a shell exploded in the cabin, riddling the fuselage with white-hot splinters. An instant later, there was a dull thud as a fuel tank in the damaged wing caught fire.

Slater knew that it was the end. He was quite calm. His action of raising his arms to cover his face, as a line of trees swept up to meet him, was purely instinctive.

Richter swept over the blazing wreck and pulled away, glancing at his watch as he did so. They had been in the Eindhoven area for five minutes; the jets would by now have made their attack and be on their way home. He pressed the R/T button, ordering his aircraft to climb through the clouds and join the others; he had a feeling that it would get unhealthy round here pretty soon.

A couple of minutes later, two sections of Tempests, led by Tim Phelan, took off from Eindhoven and climbed hard through the overcast in search of the marauders. Bursting out into brilliant sunlight at ten thousand feet, the pilots saw only a few tiny dots, rapidly dwindling into the far distance. At full boost they pursued the retreating Focke-Wulfs as far as the Rhine before giving up the chase.

On the way home, dropping down through the clouds again, they spotted a few enemy trucks, winding their way along a narrow road near Goch. Phelan led his pilots down and each made several firing passes, leaving all the German vehicles burning. It made the Irishman feel slightly better; but Ken Slater had been a good friend, and shooting up a handful of trucks in no way compensated for the fact that the Eindhoven fighters should have been airborne in time to save his neck.

Wing Commander Yeoman, he knew, was furious. From now on, the Focke-Wulf boys from Rheine could expect fireworks.

3

Yeoman stood on the dais at the end of the long wooden shack that served as Eindhoven's briefing-room and surveyed the assembled pilots of his Wing. Normally, it was his practice to begin a briefing with a quip or some comment that was designed to make his pilots feel at ease and to release the tension everyone always felt before operations; today, however, his face was grim and he came straight to the point.

'Gentlemen,' he said, 'there are indications that, for the first time in many months, the Luftwaffe is going on to the offensive. During the past few days – that is, since operational flying on both sides resumed after that appalling spell of bad weather – growing numbers of enemy fighter-bombers, and that includes jets, have been making deep penetration attacks in daylight into Allied territory. Our Intelligence people think that the Huns are up to something, but as yet they don't know what.'

He turned aside and picked up a billiard cue, tapping it against a large map of northern Germany that hung on the wall.

'The main concentration of enemy fighters and fighter-bombers is here, at Rheine, and on the various satellite airfields scattered round about. These aircraft, which are mainly Focke-Wulfs – the long-nosed variety, with a few of the earlier FW 190As – and Messerschmitt 262 jets, are grouped under the command of a single unit, Fighter Wing 66.'

Yeoman smiled thinly, then went on: 'Jagdgeschwader 66, to give it its German title, is no stranger to me personally – nor, I daresay, to a number of others in this room. It was in the thick of the fighting in France, in 1940, and in the Battle of Britain, and it cropped up later in Greece and over Malta. It is a very, very experienced outfit, and the chap who commands it is one of the enemy's top fighter leaders. His name is Colonel Richter and he has, so they say, nearly a hundred victories to his credit.'

A murmur of derision ran round the room: RAF pilots generally did not pay much attention to the claims of their German counterparts. They were unaware of the havoc the latter had wrought in Russia three years earlier against the relatively inexperienced pilots of the Soviet Air Force.

Yeoman held up his right hand to restore silence.

'All right, I know your views. But don't underestimate our friend at Rheine; the Luftwaffe's top fighter boys are good, very good indeed, and he's one of the best. What's more, you may be certain that the men under his command are the cream, too. In short, we can expect a lot of opposition from JG 66.'

The point of the billiard cue moved across the map, pausing briefly at other enemy airfields in the north-western sector as Yeoman brought his pilots up to date on the Luftwaffe's current order of battle, as compiled by the Allied Intelligence Staff. As he spoke, it quickly became clear that the fighter squadrons of the RAF's 2nd Tactical Air Force were, for the time being at least, outnumbered by their opponents across the Rhine – a situation brought about by the lack of suitable operational airfields in Belgium and Holland. Although 2nd TAF had more aircraft on paper, many of these were concentrated on airfields a long way from the front.

Yeoman made it clear to the assembled pilots that some hard fighting was certainly in store for the RAF units that were close to the front line.

'If the present trend continues,' he told them, 'we may expect to encounter large formations of enemy fighters and fighter-bombers during the weeks to come, and this will mean a complete revision of our tactics.

'Hitherto our forays into enemy territory have been carried out by sections of Tempests operating more or less independently of one another. From now on, we shall operate in two formations of six or eight aircraft, carrying out parallel sweeps with not more than fifty miles between each formation. This will ensure that if one lot runs into trouble, the other can come to its assistance fairly quickly.

'As an added insurance measure, the Spits of 449 Squadron will operate over the Rhine whenever the Tempests of 505 and 473 Squadrons carry out a sortie; in this way, they'll be able to cover us on the way out if we have to make a run for it.

'One other thing: a section of Tempests, pooled from the two squadrons, will remain at cockpit readiness at all times during daylight. I don't want any repetition of the events of the other day, when those Huns shot down the duty Anson practically under our noses and got clean away.'

Yeoman was still smarting over that incident; the failure of the Eindhoven fighters to intercept the marauding Focke-Wulfs had earned him a rocket from Group HQ, the latter having apparently ignored the fact that radar had failed to detect the enemy until it was too late.

'As I said earlier,' the Wing Commander continued, 'our Intelligence chaps are convinced that the Huns are planning something big – hence all this air activity to test our reactions, and the growing number of incursions by Messerschmitt 262 reconnaissance jets. Well, it's up to us to hit them hard, and to keep on hitting them whenever and wherever we can. As of now, our primary target is the Luftwaffe, together with its airfields.'

There were groans from the audience, many of whom saw visions of suicidal airfield attacks through a forest of anti-aircraft fire looming large before them. Yeoman recognized their apprehension, and gave a sudden disarming grin.

'Don't worry,' he said. 'We won't be attacking the airfields themselves – that is, not unless we're specifically ordered to do so. On the face of it, our main concern will still be attacks on enemy transport and communications – but every time we fly a sortie into Germany, we'll make damned certain that our route takes us close to a Hun fighter airfield. That way, operating at low level, I think we'll stand a far better chance of catching the Huns with their pants down than if we hang around for long periods in the vicinity of the enemy fields.'

He laid the billiard cue aside and stood facing them, his hands clasped behind his back. Simon Wynne-Williams, seated unobtrusively near the back of the room, permitted himself a quiet smile. The man on the dais, he thought – an experienced, confident and self-assured leader – was a far different person from the twenty-year-old boy who had arrived in France on that May day in 1940, right at the start of the German Blitzkrieg. And Wing Commander George Yeoman had yet to see his twenty-fifth birthday.

'This afternoon,' Yeoman concluded, 'we shall have an opportunity to put our new tactics to the test. Sixteen Tempests, eight from 505 Squadron and eight from 473, will attack trains in the Münster area – and on the way back we'll take a look at Rheine. Final briefing will be at 1330; take-off at 1415. That's all for now.'

The airfield was uniformly covered with a thin frosting of powdery snow, criss-crossed by the dark wheel tracks of vehicles and aircraft and by lines of footprints

Against the grey-white background, the Tempests looked darkly forbidding, as though brooding angrily over the prospect that they would soon be compelled by their masters to climb into the freezing atmosphere. Above them, shreds of grey-brown cloud trailed across a cold, eggshell-blue sky.

Yeoman, who was in No. 505 Squadron's dispersal hut with the other pilots, clasped his hands round the enamel mug to warm them and took a sip, pulling a face as the tea scalded his lips. Take-off was still ten minutes away. They would go out to their aircraft at the very last moment; there was no sense in spending unnecessarily long minutes in the cockpit, slowly freezing to the marrow.

Yeoman himself was to lead the Tempests of 505 Squadron's Red Section, with Wynne-Williams as his number two. Tim Phelan, the Squadron's rightful commander, would on this occasion lead the four Tempests of Yellow Section. Of the unit's other four fighters, two were unserviceable and Yeoman had decided to keep the other two behind on readiness at Eindhoven.

As a last check, Yeoman put through a quick call to Group Control and asked if there were any significant changes that might affect the forthcoming operation. There were none, although the weather forecasters now predicted that there was a possibility of moderate snowfalls before dark. With luck, the Tempests would all be safely home by then.

Yeoman glanced at his watch, then said quietly: 'All right, lads. Time to go.'

They picked up their parachutes, maps and flying helmets and walked out to the waiting aircraft, their boots crunching on the frosted grass. Despite the heavy clothing he was wearing Wynne-Williams shivered; even for late November, it was unnaturally cold.

He nodded to his ground crew, waiting beside the Tempest, muffled up in greatcoats and Balaclava helmets.

'Everything okay, Corporal?'

'Okay, sir. Top line.'

Wynne-Williams still found it hard to get used to the Tempest's sheer size. Handing his parachute to the corporal, he carefully inserted his fingers and toes into the spring-loaded traps built into the fighter's fuselage and climbed up to the cockpit, easing a leg over the side and balancing precariously while the airman passed the parachute up to him. Settling the pack into position, he sat down on top of it and did up his straps; parachute harness first, then seat harness, pulling the straps to make sure that they were tight. He fitted on his helmet and plugged in his R/T and oxygen leads, but left the face-mask dangling loosely for the moment.

He was not yet sufficiently familiar with the Tempest for the pre-take-off checks to be completely automatic. He went through them meticulously, one by one, muttering the sequence to himself.

'Check . . . undercarriage lever down, lever locking catch locked. Undercarriage indicator on, the green lights showing. Cockpit hood locked closed. Now, engine starting checks . . . no, wait a minute, forgotten something. Oh, yes, make sure the footstep is retracted.' He reached outside the cockpit and closed the top hand grip; that did the trick.

A glance at the ground crew to make sure they were in position, waiting.

'Right. Ignition switches off, all fuel tanks on, flaps up,

propeller speed control fully forward. Supercharger control into "M" ratio, radiator shutter down.'

Like its predecessor, the Hawker Typhoon, the Tempest employed the Koffmann starter system, which used explosive cartridges to turn the engine. The system held a total of five cartridges, so a pilot had five attempts to start a reluctant motor – in theory at least. In practice, it didn't quite work out like that; if the explosive gases of one of the cartridges failed to start the engine, there was a good chance that they would set it on fire.

Before starting the engine, he took the precaution of fastening his oxygen mask into place and turning the valve fully on, just in case poisonous fumes penetrated the cockpit. Then, satisfied that the mask was on snugly, he looked for the corporal's signal that all was clear.

The airman gave him a thumbs-up. Wynne-Williams opened the throttle gently as far as it would go, then pumped the carburettor priming handle until the fuel pressure warning light went out. Making sure the pump was screwed down, he loaded the cartridge starter by pulling a toggle on the right-hand side of the cockpit.

So far, so good. The next step was to operate the cylinder priming pump, sending a mixture of petrol and oil into the cylinders. The pump moved easily at first, then gradually stiffened under his hand. He gave it four vigorous strokes, then, with his other hand, pressed the booster coil and starter buttons simultaneously.

Slowly, creakingly, the big propeller blades began to turn over. Wynne-Williams kept the booster coil button depressed and suddenly the Sabre engine fired with a terrific bang. Immediately, an opaque film of oil spread over the windscreen. The pilot ignored it and gave the priming pump another few strokes; the engine coughed a few times and then settled down to a steady burbling roar. Breathing an involuntary sigh of relief, Wynne-Williams screwed the priming pump down and took his finger off the booster coil button.

Opening the throttle slowly, he ran the engine at 1,000 rpm and then increased the engine speed to 2,000 rpm, checking each magneto in turn and watching the oil temperatures and pressures. Next, he checked the pneumatic pressure and then the functioning of the hydraulic system by lowering and raising the flaps.

One of the ground crew, meanwhile, had climbed up on to the wing. Quickly, frozen stiff by the icy blast from the propeller, he wiped the oil from the windscreen with a clean rag, restoring the pilot's forward vision. Wynne-Williams waved at him in thanks, then completed the rest of the pre-take-off ritual, checking the operation of the supercharger and the propeller speed control.

What else? Oh, Christ, the radio! Quickly, he switched it on, and a few seconds later was rewarded by the crackle of static in his headphones.

Off to the left, Yeoman's Tempest was already starting to taxi. Wynne-Williams signalled to the ground crew to remove the chocks and released the brakes, opening the throttle until the big fighter started to move, keeping its position behind and to the right of the leader's machine.

On the perimeter track, just short of the runway, the pilots went through the check-list for take-off, using the mnemonic TPFF: 'T' for trimming tabs, 'P' for propeller pitch, 'F' for fuel settings and the other 'F' for flaps.

All set. In pairs, the Tempests moved on to the runway. A green flare arced up from the Aerodrome Control Pilot's trailer. Wynne-Williams applied too much brake as he lined up with Yeoman's aircraft and the Tempest skidded slightly on the icy surface.

He opened the throttle gradually, keeping pace with the leading aircraft as it gathered speed. Both Yeoman and he were using twenty degrees of flap, which reduced the take-off run by a hundred yards or so, but which resulted in a marked tendency to swing to the right. Wynne-Williams kept his left foot firmly pressed on the rudder pedal as the big fighter's tail came up, correcting the swing before it had time to develop properly.

The tarmac was a grey blur under the Tempest's wings. The wheels bounced once, twice, and then the fighter was airborne, the airfield falling away beneath it. Wynne-Williams touched the brakes to stop the wheels spinning – a necessary precaution, otherwise they would cause fearsome vibration as they retracted into the wings – and pulled up the undercarriage, followed by the flaps.

The Tempest formation swung round to the right, thundering over the grey slate rooftops of Eindhoven, climbing away at 185 mph on a pre-determined heading of 045 degrees. At five thousand feet they levelled out, sliding into combat formation and increasing speed to over 300 mph. Wynne-Williams stuck to Yeoman's aircraft like glue, glancing around briefly to check on the positions of the other six Tempests. A considerable distance behind, the eight aircraft of 473 Squadron were also setting course, but their track would take them farther to the south.

The 505 Squadron Tempests crossed the enemy border near Venlo and Yeoman led them down practically to ground level, the eight aircraft speeding along a hundred feet above the railway line that led to Wesel. There was no point in keeping radio silence any longer, and now Yeoman spoke for the first time.

'All right, chaps, spread out. Yellow Section, keep your eyes peeled for flak posts. Red Three and Four, watch out for fighters.'

In response to Yeoman's order, the two rearmost Tempests of Red Section popped up a couple of hundred feet, so that their pilots could make a regular scan of the sky without fear of flying into the ground or hitting some unseen obstacle. The remainder continued to search the terrain ahead, looking for trains and anything else that was worth shooting up.

As they flew on, Wynne-Williams noticed that visibility was growing steadily worse, with a grey mist creeping over the land. By the time they crossed the Rhine near Wesel – making a careful detour to avoid the formidable anti-aircraft concentrations in and around the town – the horizon was completely obscured. Above the mist, great banks of cloud, pregnant with snow, billowed up into the eastern sky, directly in front of their noses.

So far, miraculously, there had been no opposition from enemy flak. They curved around the southern outskirts of

Dorsten and picked up the railway line again, maintaining their spread-out formation. Wynne-Williams reached down and pulled a map from the top of his flying-boot; the chart was folded neatly to display the route along which they were flying and he glanced quickly along it, checking off the towns in their path: Haltern, Dülmen, the village of Buldern and then Münster itself, whose railway yards were their main objective.

'Train ahead, one o'clock.'

Yeoman's voice crackled in Wynne-Williams' headphones and he hastily shoved the map back into the top of his boot, at the same time looking ahead. Immediately, still a long way in front of the hurtling Tempests and slightly off to the right, he spotted a plume of steam, rising straight up out of the haze that covered the landscape.

Hastily, he switched on his reflector gunsight and pushed the propeller control into fine pitch, hearing the Sabre engine's dull roar change to a full-throated howl as he followed his leader down to the attack. Yeoman was already firing, dark smoke trails streaming back from the Tempest's wings. A spray of glowing coals leaped ahead of his aircraft, twinkled over the dark snake of the train that now leaped to meet the attackers out of the haze.

Wynne-Williams gave a touch of right rudder and opened fire in turn, seeing his shells rip into the rearmost of the freight cars and then ripple along towards the locomotive. He saw a sudden burst of steam, followed by black smoke.

Then the flak started to come up, God only knew from where. He hunched down lower in the cockpit and swept straight over the train at more than 400 mph, through the web of fiery tracer that reached up to claw him out of the sky. There must be a flak truck on the bloody train, he thought wildly. Then, suddenly, he was out of danger, streaking up the line in pursuit of Yeoman's Tempest.

A few seconds later, Yeoman's voice came over the air again.

'Ramrod Leader to Ramrod Aircraft. Is everybody okay?'

One by one they acknowledged. Laconically, Tim Phelan said:

'We got the train. The loco blew up.'

'Good show. Stay close, and keep your eyes open. They know we're here, now.'

The Tempests flew on towards Münster. Near Buldern they made a short detour from the railway line and attacked an enemy convoy moving along the road that ran parallel to it, a mile and a half away. Wynne-Williams had a hazy impression of explosive shells, flashing and sparkling among the dark outlines of trucks, of something erupting in a boiling bubble of smoke and flame, of wreckage, turning over and over in the air, and that was all he had time to catch before the Tempests' terrific speed took them over and away, leaving a spreading column of smoke behind them.

Less than two minutes later they swept down like a whirlwind on a marshalling yard that lay on the southern outskirts of Münster. The flak was accurate and intense and they made only one high-speed firing pass, flashing low over the intricate network of railway lines.

Wynne-Williams, ignoring the rolling stock in the sidings, selected a signal box as his target. It was a big affair, perched high above the yard, and his 20-mm shells pulverized it. A split second later he was forced to break sharply as a Tempest sheered across his nose, almost colliding with him. The aircraft, wobbling uncertainly from side to side, crashed full tilt into the signal box Wynne-Williams had just shattered. There was a terrific explosion and rivers of burning fuel licked out across the tracks.

The sky was filled with multi-coloured streamers of light now as a dozen flak posts opened up on the fleeting, twisting Tempests. Wynne-Williams sighted one of the posts, perched on top of a shed, and fired at it while still on the turn, but his shells flew wide of the mark. He passed through a pall of smoke that temporarily obscured his vision and instinctively pulled back the stick, sending the fighter rocketing skywards. Dimly over the R/T, he heard Yeoman's voice:

'Okay, chaps, let's get out of it. Reform to the north-west.'

They sped away from Münster, away from the inferno of the marshalling yard. Looking back, Wynne-Williams counted the Tempests: there were seven of them, including himself, so the aircraft that had crashed into the signal box had been the only casualty. The unfortunate machine was Red Four, flown by a sergeant pilot named Barker – one of the replacements who had arrived at Eindhoven with Wynne-Williams a few days earlier. With a sudden shock, Wynne-Williams realized that he couldn't even recall what the man had looked like.

Yeoman circled briefly to the north-west of Münster to allow the other Tempests to regain formation. As he did so, there came a sudden cry of alarm from one of the pilots in Tim Phelan's section:

'Look out! Aircraft, four o'clock high!'

Craning his neck, Wynne-Williams looked back over his right shoulder in time to see a cluster of dots a couple of miles away. Adrenalin coursed through his veins, quickly followed by a comforting surge of relief as he recognized the aggressive shapes of 473 Squadron's Tempests. The latter descended cautiously, waggling their wings to ensure identification, and fell into position a mile or so to starboard of 505 Squadron's aircraft. A few moments later, the two formations set course northwards in the direction of Rheine, remaining at low level.

They were only some fifteen miles from the enemy airfield, and so Yeoman decided to hold his present course as far as the little town of Emsdetten and then sweep sharply to the left across the approach to Rheine's main runway, keeping well clear of the enemy flak lanes. It was not long before these tactics paid dividends. As the Tempest formation swung to the left, a Junkers 52 transport aircraft lumbered directly across its path. The Ju 52 sheered away from the threat and made a desperate attempt to reach Bentlage, one of Rheine's small satellite airfields, but a section of 473 Squadron pounced on it and shot it flaming into a wood.

Apart from the solitary Junkers, the sky was empty of enemy machines. After several fruitless minutes quartering the sky to the south and west of Rheine, Yeoman finally gave up and ordered the Tempests to set course for home. He was worried about the weather, which by this time was deteriorating rapidly. Heavy clouds had completely obliterated the sun and a strange, leaden twilight was falling over the land. Although it was relatively warm in the Tempest's cockpit Yeoman felt a shiver run down his spine.

The fighters' homeward course took them over more or less open country, dotted with woods and villages. Yet there was menace even here; more than once, flak rose to meet them from seemingly-innocuous country lanes, or from gun posts on the outskirts of innocent hamlets. The Tempests jinked away from it, their high speed carrying them out of danger.

Hurtling across the ground at 350 mph and almost at tree-top height was a nerve-racking business, yet strangely enough Wynne-Williams felt a curious sense of detachment as he clung like a limpet to Yeoman's Tempest, following every move his leader made. There was something unreal about it all: the leaden, lowering sky, the drab, grey-green landscape that was little more than a blur, the dull thunder of the big engine. He had the oddest feeling that he was plunging down-hill out of control, that any second he would smash headlong into a great brick wall that would somehow materialize out of the mist on the horizon.

He shook his head in an attempt to dispel the weird illusion and checked his oxygen flow. It was functioning normally. Yet the strange detachment persisted, accompanied now by a sense of oppression, as though earth and clouds were closing in like grim walls to trap and crush him.

'Rhine ahead. Look out for shipping.'

With something approaching panic welling up inside him, Wynne-Williams strove to pull his scattered senses together. Peering ahead through the hazy blur of the propeller, he made out the dull grey expanse of the great river, sliced across by bridges. Crawling under one of the bridges was a long string of barges, their outlines blurred in the murk.

Yeoman opened fire, followed by Wynne-Williams a fraction of a second later. Cannon shells churned up the water, crept across to the line of barges and obscured them with flying spray. As he swept overhead, Wynne-Williams noted with complete detachment that one of the barges had a string of multi-coloured washing fluttering from a line rigged along the length of its deck.

The Tempests were coming under fire now from 20-mm flak batteries on the west bank of the Rhine, the barrels of their guns depressed to as low an angle as possible. The gunners pumped clip after clip of shells into the path of the Tempests, heedless of the fact that some of their missiles were exploding among the barges that were moving steadily along the waterway close to the opposite bank. The latter came under attack from the Tempests of 473 Squadron and were soon holed and sinking, joining those which had been hit seconds earlier by 505 Squadron's aircraft.

Racing away from the river, Wynne-Williams used up the last of his ammunition against a flak tower, the top of which vanished in an explosion of powdered masonry. A village passed under his wings and he had a hazy glimpse of people hurling themselves into doorways as his aircraft zipped a few feet above their heads.

All the Tempests were over the Rhine now, heading out over the last few miles of German territory and into Holland. They passed to the south of the enemy airfield at Laarbruch and kept a watchful eye on the sky, but no German fighters were in the air and, in any case, few of the Tempests still had ammunition.

The weather was closing in rapidly now, and as they crossed the River Maas the pilots strained their eyes to pick out familiar landmarks, for Holland – flat and featureless, criss-crossed with its maze of waterways – was not the easiest of countries for visual navigation. Then the Helmond–Venlo railway line came up ahead and they curved across it to the right, picking up Eindhoven without difficulty. Ten minutes later all fifteen Tempests were safely on the ground and taxi-ing to their dispersals.

Wynne-Williams swung the nose of his aircraft into wind and opened the throttle to 1,000 rpm, keeping an eye on the blue smoke that flowed back from the exhaust stubs. When it died away to a trickle and finally ceased altogether, it meant that surplus oil had been expelled from the engine. Satisfied at length that all was well, he pulled the cut-out lever and the rumble of the engine died away as the propeller flicked to a standstill.

He switched off the ignition and fuel, then opened the cockpit canopy, thankfully unfastening his oxygen mask and pulling off his helmet. The air was bitter, with drops of freezing moisture in it, and stung his sweaty face.

He unfastened his harness and clambered down from the cockpit, pulling his parachute pack after him and dropping it into the arms of one of his ground crew. The airman looked at him anxiously.

'Are you all right, sir?' he asked. The pilot nodded.

'Well, you've collected some holes. Just there, sir, look.'

The man pointed to a spot just behind the cockpit. A line of ragged holes scarred the fuselage roundel. Wynne-Williams swallowed hard; a couple of feet further forward, and the bullets would have perforated him.

The ground crew corporal came round the end of the wing and looked at the holes reprovingly, as though suggesting that the pilot might have looked after the aircraft better. Then he turned to Wynne-Williams and grinned suddenly.

'Good trip, sir? Did you get anything?'

'We shot up a few trains,' the pilot answered, 'and some barges on the Rhine. Oh – and the 473 Squadron boys clobbered a Junkers 52. But there wasn't much doing, really.'

He turned away and walked over to join Yeoman, who had paused to light his pipe – which always flew with him on operations, packed and ready to be lit – a few yards away from his Tempest. He looked up as Wynne-Williams approached.

'Well, Simon, that was your first long sortie into Indian territory. What did you think of it?'

Wynne-Williams scratched an itchy spot on his cheek, where his oxygen mask had chafed him.

'This low-level-all-the-way stuff takes a bit of getting used to, doesn't it? I felt decidedly queasy at one point – claustrophobic almost, just as though things were closing in around me.'

Yeoman smiled. 'You probably got a bit disorientated,' he said. 'Nothing to worry about. You sometimes get funny impressions, when you're flying low and fast, especially if the visibility is marginal and there's no horizon. The thing to do is concentrate on your instruments for a few seconds; that usually does the trick. You'll get used to it.'

'The flak was pretty bad,' Wynne-Williams commented. His companion gave a derisory laugh.

'Bad? That was bugger all, my friend. Just wait until we

carry out an airfield attack to find out what flak's really like! One of the Typhoon squadrons attacked Laarbruch a few weeks ago, and lost eight out of twelve.'

'Not exactly a comforting thought,' Wynne-Williams murmured, as they walked towards the debriefing hut. There, for the next ten minutes, the Wing's Intelligence Officers quizzed them on the afternoon's events: targets attacked, opposition encountered, anything of special significance observed, and so on.

The pilots clamoured eagerly round the trestle tables, clutching mugs of tea and gratefully inhaling cigarette smoke, anxious to tell their stories and then board the truck that was to take them into Eindhoven. Now that the tension of the sortie had dissipated, they were ravenously hungry; even half-burnt sausages and dehydrated potato would be welcome.

One of their number stood at the window, a half-smoked cigarette between his fingers, staring moodily out over the airfield. He was thinking of Sergeant Barker, who had been his room-mate and whose charred, unrecognizable remains now lay under the wreckage of his Tempest on the outskirts of Münster. In his mind's eye, he could picture the report on the operation that would end up in the files of 83 Group, written by some dispassionate wingless wonder who had probably never been near an aeroplane:

'Wednesday, 29 November 1944. Offensive sortie by sixteen Tempests of 505 and 473 Squadrons, Eindhoven. Trains attacked in the Münster area. One Junkers 52 destroyed (by 473 Squadron) on approach to Rheine. Barges attacked on the Rhine in Wesel area. Moderate flak encountered; no enemy fighter activity. One Tempest (505 Squadron) failed to return.'

There it was, in four or five cryptic lines: the everyday life of a Tempest squadron.

Outside, it was beginning to snow. There would be no flying while it snowed. The young pilot at the window hoped that it would snow forever.

4

The snowfall did not continue. After brief showers that fell on and off for two days it ceased altogether, leaving the countryside dusted with powdery particles of ice.

After the snow came the fog, spreading its dirty grey blanket over the land, more surely and swiftly halting air operations than any other kind of bad weather. At Eindhoven and the other forward airfields on the 2nd Tactical Air Force's front, while the Tempests, Typhoons and Spitfires stood earthbound like grey ghosts on their freezing dispersals, the pilots took advantage of the unexpected respite to relax as best they could.

Mostly they slept – or tried to sleep, for sleep does not come easily to a body whose nerves are bunched into knots by the incessant strain of flying a high-performance combat aircraft at low level into the teeth of murderous flak, knowing that one's chances of survival are no more than fifty per cent. When they did manage to sleep, they often awoke feeling more wretched than before, and the sleeping pills provided for them by their medical officers offered no real solution.

The makeshift bar in the convent-cum-mess in Eindhoven stayed open from twelve noon until midnight and there was no shortage of beer and spirits, but it was a rare thing to find more than half a dozen pilots gathered there at any one time, and even then their purpose was usually to play cards, chess or draughts, rather than to drink. The same pilots, when they were on duty, reported conscientiously to the airfield every morning – and played cards, chess or draughts in their dispersal huts until darkness fell. Quite a few of the pilots had formed relationships with hospitable Dutch families in

Eindhoven, and many a tin of corned beef and packet of tea found its way on to kitchen tables to supplement a grateful housewife's own meagre rations.

Yeoman spent the first day and a half of the fog in clearing up a deskful of outstanding paperwork that required his attention, and in reading all the latest Intelligence reports. Privately, he was worried about the state of morale of the Eindhoven Wing; the pilots' apathy and general listlessness were becoming all too apparent, and the last straw came when he organized a rugger match against the Typhoon boys from Gilze and then, through lack of interest on the part of his men, only just succeeded in getting together a XV which the Typhoon boys beat by forty points to three.

The following morning, on Yeoman's orders, every pilot not on duty went for a five-mile cross-country run. They returned, panting, cursing and mud-spattered, to find that soccer matches had been arranged for the afternoon, and that anyone not wishing to take part could go on another cross-country run with the kind co-operation of the physical training officer of a nearby army unit. Everyone decided to take part. A notice on the mess board proclaimed that the programme would be repeated the next day, and for as long as the bad weather continued.

That night, the bar was full. Yeoman stood in a corner near the stove and quietly smoked his pipe, exchanging an occasional comment with Tim Phelan. He was aware of sidelong glances from one or two of his pilots, and was also aware that they probably considered him to be a bastard with a capital B. He didn't care; the Wing was beginning to come together again as a team, and that was all that mattered.

And so, still under its foggy shroud, the war slipped into its sixth December, and all along the front, from the Hook of Holland to the junction of the German, French and Swiss borders, the Allied Command began the concentration of massive forces at strategic points so that when all was ready, they could resume the attack with a series of smashing blows designed to bring Germany finally to her knees. Already, the US Third Army had reached the River Saar at four points, and the stage seemed set for the last great offensive.

The enemy, however, was not finished yet, as the Allies – and in particular the Americans – were soon to discover to their cost.

At night and under cover of the blanket of fog, safe from the omnipresent eyes of the Allied reconnaissance aircraft, a thousand tanks and a quarter of a million men – equal to twelve divisions – had been moving steadily up to assembly areas in the eastern fringes of the Ardennes, that great natural barrier of dense pine forests, deep ravines, steep ridges and fast-flowing streams sprawling over the common frontiers of Germany, Belgium and Luxembourg.

The creation of this massive force of men and armour had been little short of a miracle. During November 1944 war production in Germany had broken all records in order to turn it into a reality, and an entire new army group had been formed by scraping the bottom of the manpower barrel to conscript sixteen-year-old boys, middle-aged men and those who had hitherto been considered medically unfit.

So, early in December, three armies – one armoured and two infantry – were stealthily moved into the Eifel hills, facing an eighty-five-mile sector of the American front running from Monschau in the north through the Ardennes to Echternach in Luxembourg – a sector defended by only four divisions of the US VIII Corps, of which two had never been tested in combat and two were recuperating after receiving a terrible mauling in savage forest fighting a couple of weeks earlier.

The new German force was designated Army Group B and was commanded by Feldmarschall Walter Model, a soldier of vast experience who believed that attack was the best form of defence and whose aggressive tactics had saved the German armies on the Eastern Front from crushing defeat on three occasions. The generals under his command were equally experienced and battle-hardened; men like General Josef 'Sepp' Dietrich, who had actually been Hitler's sergeant-major in the First World War and whose Sixth SS Panzer Army was to spearhead the offensive in the north; and like General Hasso von Manteuffel, a small, hawk-faced man – also a veteran of the terrible battles in Russia – whose Fifth Panzer

Army was to attack through the centre, protected on its long southern flank by the infantry of the newly-raised Seventh Army.

The German plan was to be virtually a carbon copy of the Blitzkrieg of May 1940. Following a massive artillery barrage, assault troops would smash the weak American defensive line in several places, creating gaps through which the armour and infantry would pour, flooding the Ardennes to capture key bridges over the Meuse.

Once this first phase of the offensive had been completed, and before the Allies could regain their composure, Army Group B would then drive north-westward to the vital port of Antwerp, where it would be joined by the Fifteenth Army under General Kurt Student – the redoubtable paratroop commander whose men had captured Crete three and a half years earlier – pushing southwards from Holland. Between them, Army Group B and the Fifteenth Army would secure Antwerp and the Scheldt Estuary, driving a great wedge through the Allied armies and destroying the four that would then be trapped in the northern pocket – the US 1st and 9th, the British 2nd and the Canadian 1st.

It was the firm belief of Adolf Hitler that once this objective had been achieved, the western Allies would be more than ready to sue for peace, leaving the Germans free to send all their forces into the battle against the Russians. His generals were not so optimistic. Feldmarschall von Rundstedt – who would later be erroneously named as the architect of the operation – was outspoken in his condemnation of it, right from the outset. Hitler, however, was adamant that it should go ahead; after two postponements, he decreed that the offensive should begin not later than dawn on 16 December.

The final Blitzkrieg was to go ahead, despite all opposition. And as the build-up of troops and armour continued, so the morale of the German troops and their commanders slowly but surely lifted. Perhaps the Führer was right; perhaps they could still snatch a victory from defeat, avenging the shattered cities of the Fatherland and the hundreds of thousands of Germans who had died. And if not . . . would it not be better to end in horror, than to face a horror without end?

Oberstleutnant Joachim Richter was not one of the optimistic ones. On Sunday, 10 December, after attending a briefing on the forthcoming operation – which was code-named 'Autumn Fog' – he quietly confessed his misgivings to Oberstleutnant Erwin Wiltz, an old friend from the days before the war who now commanded a fighter-bomber wing.

'I know the Ardennes, Erwin, just as you do yourself. Remember those twisting, turning roads? Why, pushing tanks and trucks over them was difficult enough in 1940, when it was summer – and now they plan to do the same thing in the middle of winter, when the roads will be waist deep in snow.' He shook his head. 'It's just not feasible.'

Wiltz chuckled. 'And all this at Christmas time, too, just to make things worse.'

His face grew serious and he thoughtfully swirled the cognac round in his glass. Richter noticed the deep lines etched on his companions's forehead, the streaks of grey in his hair, though he was not yet thirty years old.

'Seriously, Joachim,' he went on soberly, 'what alternative is there? To pull all our forces in and concentrate on defending the perimeter of the Fatherland? You know that wouldn't work. We could probably hold the enemy for a time, but in the end they would starve us into submission. We'd have no fuel or raw materials left, or food either. The whole of Germany would become one vast charnel house.'

'Some people would prefer to see it that way,' Richter said softly, 'rather than live with defeat.'

Wiltz looked up, studying the other's face intently, and gave a tired smile.

'I know what you mean, Jo. We know that the Führer does not think the German race fit to survive in defeat. But I don't happen to agree with all this Wagnerian "Twilight of the Gods" nonsense. I have two children in Bavaria, and I want them to grow up – hopefully into a better world than the one you and I have known.'

He set aside his glass and sat back in his chair. The two of them were quite alone in the apartment, which belonged to Wiltz' brother – a Panzer major who was at present somewhere in northern Italy. It was small but comfortably furnished, and Wiltz had the use of it whenever he happened to be in the capital. He noticed with dissatisfaction that there was a large crack in the ceiling, the result of vibrations set up by Allied bombing. In fact, it was little short of miraculous that the apartment had survived this far without serious damage.

'I believe that we must make one last great effort,' he continued, 'even though we might exhaust our forces in the west in the process. Total collapse on the Western Front, after all, will only result in the Tommies and Amis reaching Berlin a lot faster – and I'd rather see them here than the Ivans.'

In this, Richter was in total agreement. He shuddered to think what would happen if the Russians, bloodthirsty for revenge, ever set foot on the soil of Germany.

'This offensive, as I see it, is our last chance – our sole remaining chance – to make the Allies see sense,' Wiltz emphasized. 'We must make them see how costly it will be for them if they fail to agree to a compromise. And, Jo, don't forget that we have one factor on our side – the Allies must be as sick and tired of this war as we are ourselves.'

Richter lit one of his customary cheroots and peered at Wiltz through the drifting cloud of grey smoke.

'Do you really think this offensive has a chance of success?' There was a cynical note as he asked the question. Wiltz spread out his hands.

'I wish I could say "yes" with certainty,' he said. 'But who can tell? So much depends on so many different factors. Speed and surprise . . . the ability of our spearhead forces to capture Allied fuel dumps so that the armour can keep moving . . . and, of course, the weather.'

'Yes, the weather,' Richter agreed. 'That's the key factor. The forecast for mid-December is fog and snow. If it's accurate, then we might have a chance after all. The going will be hard, but at least snow and fog will keep the Allied air forces on the ground. We don't want the whole operation to end in another Falaise,' he concluded grimly.

Wiltz nodded. The Germans had bitter memories of those grim days in August, when thousands of troops and masses of transport, in full retreat through the Falaise gap, had been wiped out by the continual onslaught of Allied fighter-bombers.

Richter hoped against hope that the weather forecast was right, and that the fog of the last few days – which had given way to cold, intermittent rain – would return. He did not envy the lot of the thousands of Wehrmacht troops who would soon be trudging through the Ardennes in the teeth of winter, weary and soaking wet, lashed by freezing particles of snow and sleet, knowing that they would have to go for days without proper sleep, fighting incessantly and sustained only by the knowledge that the success of this last, desperate gamble depended on their fortitude. Suddenly, he felt ashamed to be sitting in this comfortable apartment in the glow of the firelight, his belly warmed by good food and cognac. He thought of all the thousands who would die, of all the thousands who had already died; boys who were little more than children, young men and old; the past, the present and the future of Germany, severed from the body of their motherland as though by a surgeon's knife and cast into oblivion.

And he knew, suddenly, that whatever the outcome of this last offensive might be, the end for Germany would be the same; for the future was gone, wantonly sacrificed to the gods of war.

5

An insistent voice was penetrating Yeoman's dreams. He tried to ignore it but it refused to go away, and now someone was shaking him, tearing aside the warm, comforting canopy of sleep.

He stuck his head out from under the blankets and opened one eye, then closed it again quickly as the harsh light of a torch seared it.

'What's the matter?' he grunted. The voice that answered him was that of the duty officer.

'Group Control's just been on the phone, sir. They want us to put on a maximum-effort sweep as far as Bremen. Take off at first light.'

Yeoman propped himself up on one elbow, carefully keeping the blankets around him to hold in the warmth.

'Bremen? That's a bloody long way. What time is it, anyway?'

'Four o'clock, sir.'

'Oh, shit. All right, thanks for telling me. I'll be along directly.'

The duty officer left the room and Yeoman promptly dozed off again, knowing that in fifteen minutes' time the amazing McGann, ever on the alert, would visit him with a mug of scalding tea and a couple of thick bacon sandwiches. McGann, who looked after the two squadron commanders and a couple of flight lieutenants as well as Yeoman, seemed to have a sixth sense about a forthcoming operation and was always up and about a good half-hour before anyone else, his kettle burbling away on the stove.

'Guidmornin', sorr. Here's yer tea an' yer saanies.'

The tubby Scot's voice jerked Yeoman wide awake and he sat up in bed, reaching out for the mug. It was freezing cold in his room, and he was grateful for the warmth that seeped through the enamel into his fingers.

'Good morning to you, Jock. What's the weather like?'

'Jest a wee bit frosty, sorr. Sky's pretty clear, though. It'll snow afore dark,' he added cheerfully.

Yeoman nodded and sat for a few moments lost in thought, sipping his tea and munching his sandwiches, waiting for McGann to return with his bucket of hot water. The batman's 'wee bit frosty' probably meant that the temperature was way below freezing, which in turn meant that there would be the usual crop of problems in starting the Tempests' engines and in taking off on icy runways.

He got out of bed and did a few physical exercises to warm himself up, then washed and shaved quickly in the water McGann brought him. He dressed hurriedly, before the cold had time to seize him, putting on the heaviest clothing he had; long woollen underpants, thick socks, a fisherman's jersey over the top of his uniform shirt. Pulling on his trousers, he tucked the bottoms into the woollen socks and inserted his feet with some difficulty into his flying-boots. Then he wriggled into his battledress blouse, into the pockets of which he stuffed two bars of chocolate, a box of matches, his pipe and tobacco.

He took his Smith and Wesson .38 revolver from its holster, which was hanging behind the bedroom door, and checked that it was loaded before wedging it firmly into the top of his right flying-boot. Finally, after drinking the last dregs of his tea, he picked up his cap and made his way downstairs.

He reached the dining-room and, hanging his cap on a nail which somebody had hammered into the wall outside the door, went inside. The dining room, shared by officers and NCOs alike, must once have been the nuns' refectory; it was furnished with two long tables and hard, wooden benches.

Yeoman sat down opposite Tim Phelan and Squadron Leader Vincent Masters, 473 Squadron's commander, and gave a nondescript grunt that might have meant 'good morning'. They grunted back at him and said nothing else, being fully aware that their wing commander hated early morning attempts at conversation and, in fact, that he was not generally fit to live with until something like eight o'clock.

The room was beginning to fill up as pilots trudged in and plonked themselves down wordlessly on the hard benches. Sleepy airmen hovered around them, doling out helpings of fried bacon, greasy sausages, and scrambled powdered egg that tasted, as Phelan put it, like the inside of a wrestler's jockstrap. Yeoman would have given his right arm for a fresh, golden egg, but nobody had seen a hen for weeks. Instead, he opted for a bowl of porridge; it was hot and filling and, with some sugar on it, was at least palatable. That and the bacon he'd just eaten would sustain him until his next meal. He was pleased to see that all the other pilots seemed to be eating heartily; he had constantly stressed the need to fill one's stomach before flying, no matter how much one lacked an appetite. A man with a full stomach flew better, fought better and thought faster.

Their transport arrived a few minutes later and they went out into the freezing darkness. Yeoman, Phelan and Masters climbed into Yeoman's Mercedes, which, with headlights masked, led the small convoy over the slippery roads to the airfield. It was impossible to see more than a couple of yards ahead, and Yeoman told his driver to proceed with caution. Only two days earlier, a jeep carrying a load of 449 Squadron pilots, travelling too fast, had skidded off the icy road. The result: one pilot dead, with his neck broken, and another with crushed legs.

They arrived at the airfield without incident and, while the other pilots went to their dispersals, Yeoman headed for the operations trailer with Phelan and Masters to find out what was going on.

It was pleasantly warm inside the trailer. Makeshift curtains were drawn to prevent the escape of light and a paraffin heater was going full blast. The duty pilot stood up as Yeoman and the others entered; he looked as though he had been asleep. Yeoman nodded to him and reached for the telephone, putting through a call to Group Central Control.

The voice on the other end of the line belonged to Squadron Leader Gordon Latimer, who was GCC's duty controller this morning. Yeoman was secretly pleased, for Latimer knew his job inside out and would be certain to steer the Tempests towards any 'trade', if indeed there was any.

'Good morning, Gordon,' Yeoman said. 'What's the gen?'

'Morning, sir. Sorry to get you up at this unearthly hour, but we've had reports that fairly strong Luftwaffe fighter formations have just moved into airfields in the Bremen area, notably Delmenhorst and Lemwerder. We'd like you to take a look at the situation at first light and see if you can catch a few of the Huns unawares.'

'How strong exactly are the Luftwaffe units?'

'Three or four Gruppen – about fifty to sixty aircraft, mostly Focke-Wulfs. Our Intelligence people think they've been withdrawn from the Eastern Front. It reinforces their belief that the Huns are planning some sort of big show.'

'All right, Gordon.' Yeoman looked at his watch. 'We'll take off at seven-thirty. I'll give you a ring in a few minutes and let you know how many aircraft we have available.'

The Tempest Wing's state of serviceability was not particularly good, as Yeoman learned a few minutes later from Warrant Officer Booth, the senior engineer NCO. Out of twelve aircraft per squadron, No. 505 had eight airworthy machines and No. 473 only seven. There was a possibility, he said, that two more Tempests could be made available before take-off time.

'I'm sorry, sir,' he apologized, 'it seems to be just one of those bloody days. My lads have been working like beavers, but one snag after another has cropped up. Those Sabre engines don't like the cold weather.'

'All right, Mr Booth,' Yeoman said gently. 'I know you'll do your best.'

He could ask for no more; he knew that the Wing's ground crews were among the best to be found anywhere and that here, on one of the most inhospitable of 2nd TAF's front-line airfields, they were compelled to work under appalling conditions in order to keep the fighters flying. Yet, although there were the usual grumbles, they did their job to the best of their ability, and there were never any serious complaints.

Warrant Officer Booth was as good as his word. By seven o'clock the Wing's total of serviceable Tempests had risen to seventeen. Now, in the pre-dawn darkness, Eindhoven was a flurry of activity as the ground crews busied themselves around the aircraft, working under dim lights hastily rigged up and powered by diesel generators, running up the engines, checking and re-checking the systems to make sure that everything was in full working order.

At 0720 the Tempests began taxi-ing out towards the faint lights of the flarepath. A grey, wintry dawn was already beginning to spread over the eastern horizon and the taxi-ing aircraft showed up darkly against it, their outlines given an unreal appearance by the glow of their navigation lights and the ghostly blue flames that crackled from their exhaust stubs.

Yeoman taxied on to the runway, looked round quickly to check that the other Tempests were getting into position, and opened the throttle to start his take-off run. Once again, Simon Wynne-Williams was flying as his number two. The burned pilot, Yeoman thought, had dropped back into squadron life with surprising ease and showed that he had lost none of his old skill. This would be his seventh operational flight in a Tempest; over the past fortnight he had badgered Yeoman to be allowed to fly at every opportunity, whenever there had been the slightest break in the weather, and on his last trip he had shot down a Junkers 88 at dusk over Nordhorn, near the Dutch border. One of the squadron's flight commanders was due for a rest soon, and Yeoman had already decided that Wynne-Williams should take his place, now that he had found his feet again.

Once the Tempests were safely airborne and had settled down on course in their combat formation, Yeoman switched off his navigation lights well before they entered enemy territory. It was now light enough to keep formation without their aid, and already the metallic snake of the River Maas and other details of the terrain ahead were beginning to manifest themselves out of the twilight.

The Tempests thundered on at two thousand feet. There was some mist lying in hollows beyond the Maas, but visibility was generally good, details appearing sharp and clear as a bloated red sun pushed its rim up into the frosty sky. Once, off to the left, Yeoman spotted a plume of steam that indicated the presence of a train, but resisted the urge to send off a section to attack it; this morning the Tempests were after enemy fighters, not trains.

Yeoman held the control column lightly, anticipating and correcting the Tempest's tendency to roll. To conserve fuel, the formation cruised at 220 mph – a dangerously low speed in the vicinity of strong flak concentrations, but Yeoman had been careful to choose a route that avoided these.

The sun climbed higher and he lowered his smoked goggles, turning its piercing rays to a dull pink. The Tempests rocked gently as they passed under the bases of towering cumulus clouds, mountainous piles of vapour whose colours, in the early morning light, varied from pale grey to deep orange.

The Tempests passed Rheine to the north and speared deeper into Germany, hurtling over densely wooded hillsides. The area was criss-crossed by innumerable streams and small roads; navigation here depended on accurate dead-reckoning and Yeoman checked his watch frequently, counting off the seconds towards their first turning-point.

A village flashed by, a mile or so to starboard. Just to the north-east of it, beside a wood, a fine old house lay in ruins.

Yeoman knew every detail of that house, and of the village of Berge. The house had once been used by the Abwehr, the German counter-espionage service, to hold captured agents of the Allied Special Operations Executive.

Yeoman had never learned what kind of specialized knowledge those agents had possessed. He had simply been given his orders, and had led the Mosquitos of No. 380 Squadron, which he then commanded, in a gallant and devastating low-level attack on the building. No one, agents and interrogators alike, could possibly have survived.

It was as well for Yeoman's peace of mind that one fragment of knowledge had been denied him on the orders of high authority. One of the agents held captive in that house was a young American woman named Julia Connors. She was one of SOE's top operatives, but of course Yeoman had never known that. In the four years they had known one another she had maintained her cover well; he had never questioned her story that she was a correspondent for a newspaper, the *New York*

Globe, a job that took her away on lengthy assignments

They had arranged to meet in London early in October, when they were to have been married. But Julia had not come, and Yeoman had known days in an agony of suspense and anxiety – emotions that had given way to dull shock and black despair when, at last, he received the news that she had been posted missing, believed killed, while on an assignment close to the front line with the American forces in France.

The story had been carefully concocted by SOE, and Yeoman had seen no reason to doubt it. After that, he had permitted himself no time for dark brooding; instead, he had put in a request for an immediate return to operations, and it had been granted.

He looked across at Berge as it receded into the background. Half his old squadron lay shattered somewhere among those wooded hillsides; every one of those who survived had been decorated, and he himself had received the DSO.

He swung the formation round to the right, past the twin towns of Dinklage and Lohne. So far there had been no sign of enemy aircraft, but the Tempests' route was now taking them between the enemy fighter airfields of Ahlhorn and Diepholz and the head of every pilot was turning continually, searching all quarters of the sky. Yeoman made sure that his cannon safety catch was off and switched on his reflector sight.

After a few more miles he brought the formation round to the left, past Wistringen. Bremen was fifteen miles to the north. He looked over to the right, where the bottom edge of the sun was now clearing the horizon, peering into its light through outstretched fingers. There seemed to be nothing in that direction.

'Ramrod Blue Two, look out, Huns above, five o'clock!'

So Jerry was awake after all! Yeoman twisted his head round to the right, looking above and behind, turning his aircraft slightly to get a better view, and saw the enemy almost immediately. There were thirty or forty of them, slipping down between the clouds in a rather ragged attack formation towards the Tempests. They were still some miles away and it was impossible to say, at this distance, if they were Messerschmitts or Focke-Wulfs.

As always in these situations, time seemed to slow down for Yeoman, and his brain functioned with utter clarity. He made a mental note to compliment Ramrod Blue Two, who had spotted the Huns in good time and so given him those few extra seconds in which to decide on an appropriate course of action. He pressed the R/T button and said rapidly:

'Ramrod Red and Yellow Sections, stand by to break right. Blue and Green Sections, stand by to break left. Break hard into the Huns on my signal. Jettison auxiliary tanks – now!'

The pilots pulled their jettison levers and thirty-four drop tanks curved down from beneath the Tempests' wings to smash themselves on the German countryside. There were no hangups, thank God, Yeoman thought fleetingly. He glanced quickly over his shoulder again; the enemy fighters were closing the range with phenomenal speed, thanks to the impetus of their dive, and were now identifiable as Focke-Wulfs. He waited, forcing himself to hold the formation level while he coolly judged the distance between the opposing aircraft. Best not to cut it too fine . . .

'Stand by to break – *now*!'

Yeoman pushed open the throttle with one hand and pulled the stick hard into his right thigh with the other. The engine gave a great surge of power and the Tempest curved up and around in the opposite direction, half turning on its back as it gained height. The 'g' force thrust Yeoman hard down in his seat and he gave an involuntary gasp as he pushed the stick over again, rolling out of the violent climbing turn, ruddering hard and opening fire, a fraction of a second too late, as a Focke-Wulf sped past his nose.

The sudden manoeuvre by the Tempests, with the seventeen aircraft breaking hard at the last minute and rocketing upwards in a climbing turn, nine aircraft in one direction and eight in the other like the cascading waters of a fountain, had taken the enemy completely by surprise and the Focke-Wulfs scattered in all directions as their attack lost its cohesion.

Still at full throttle, and followed by the faithful Wynne-Williams, Yeoman took his Tempest in an arrowing climb to eight thousand feet and looked around for a target, finding time to shout a warning over the radio, telling his pilots not to be drawn into combat above ten thousand feet, where the Focke-Wulfs could out-manoeuvre them.

A long-nosed Focke-Wulf was turning lazily a couple of thousand feet lower down, waggling his wings in an uncertain manner. Yeoman called Wynne-Williams over the radio and told him that he was going down after the enemy aircraft.

The enemy pilot saw the danger at the last moment and threw his aircraft into a steep dive. It was precisely the wrong manoeuvre, for the much heavier Tempest could easily outpace him. Yeoman, confident that Wynne-Williams would guard his tail against any danger, gave all his concentration to the Focke-Wulf as it drifted into the luminous diamonds of his gunsight; apart from weaving gently from one side to the other the enemy pilot was taking no evasive action and Yeoman had no difficulty in keeping him lined up nicely.

The Focke-Wulf levelled out and sped low along the line of a road, heading north. Yeoman realized that the German pilot was probably making for Bremen, in an attempt to shake off his pursuers among the town's formidable anti-aircraft defences. He never made it. Yeoman's four cannon thumped briefly and he saw three distinct flashes as his shells struck home in the 190's port wing. The enemy fighter sheered brutally to the right, ripped through a row of telegraph poles and blew up in a field.

'Look out, Ramrod Leader, 190s coming down hard astern!'

Wynne-Williams' urgent voice snapped Yeoman into instinctive reaction and he climbed flat out, looking back to locate the new threat. Three long-nosed 190s were coming down towards him in a diving turn, one of them lagging a little way behind the rest.

'Ramrod Red Two, attacking.'

He caught a brief glimpse of Wynne-Williams' Tempest hurtling head-on towards the leading pair of 190s, then felt a terrific bang as something exploded in his starboard wing. He kicked the rudder frantically, slewing his fighter away from the new threat. Tracers flickered past him and an instant later the black shadow of a Focke-Wulf flashed over his cockpit canopy with only feet to spare.

He glanced quickly behind, ensuring that the sky was clear,

then went after the enemy fighter, which had pulled out of its dive and was starting to climb. He fired, missed, corrected his aim, and although he couldn't be certain he thought that his second short burst must have struck home. There was no smoke or flame from the enemy aircraft, but it suddenly came out of its climb and went into a wide spiral dive. It levelled out a few hundred feet above the ground. Yeoman followed, skimming over copses and fields at close on 450 mph, and fired again, seeing his shells plough up fountains of dirt close to the 190's wingtip. White contrails streamed back from the Focke-Wulf's wingtips as the German pilot threw the fighter into a violent turn.

Yeoman saw the 190 shudder visibly under the effects of a high-speed stall, and for a fleeting instant had a mental image of the doomed enemy pilot desperately trying to correct his error. He was too late, and too low. The Focke-Wulf turned right over on its back and its nose dropped with sickening finality. A moment later the usual mushroom cloud of black smoke, shot with bubbles of blazing petrol vapour, marked its end.

Yeoman sped over the wreck and stayed low, turning this way and that, searching the sky on all sides. The radio was filled with the excited chatter of his pilots as they locked in combat with the other 190s, but apart from some smoke trails slashed across the sky a long way away there was no evidence of the big battle that was still raging. His pursuit of the Focke-Wulf must have carried him far from the centre of the action.

He turned left, the ground blurring under his wings, intending to climb back to rejoin the others, and pressed the R/T transmit button.

'Ramrod Red Two, this is Ramrod Leader. Come in please.'

There was no answer. Yeoman opened his mouth to try again, and at that moment the sky around him was suddenly filled with blinding light as flak of every calibre opened up from all sides.

In a timeless, terror-filled fraction of a second he realized that he had inadvertently blundered into the flak lane that led to the approach of Delmenhorst airfield. He sensed, rather than felt or heard, his Tempest being hit time and time again.

He knew in that instant that his only chance was to stay as low as possible, straight and level, and make a run for it; to turn in any direction would mean exposing the large area of the Tempest's wings to the anti-aircraft gunners.

His highly-trained reflexes came into play and he pushed the throttle lever right forward through the 'gate', the metal thread that enabled him to obtain emergency power from the Tempest's engine. There was a thunderous roar and the fighter plane leaped forward, the acceleration pinning Yeoman back in his seat as the engine wound up to 3,700 rpm and the speed increased frighteningly. With the airspeed indicator showing over 500 mph the Tempest streaked through the flak zone, its pilot crouched low in the cockpit as the inferno of shellfire continued to erupt around him.

There was a terrific crash and a blast of freezing air as something smashed through his cockpit canopy, shattering the instrument panel and sending razor-edged splinters lashing into his face and hands. He cried out in pain and panic, fearing for his eyes and throwing up a protective arm, then realized that he could still see and steadied the speeding aircraft, holding his course.

Away to the left he caught a hazy, blurred glimpse of some camouflaged hangars and a long strip of concrete that showed signs of having been severely bombed. There was another loud bang as a large shell – probably a 37-mm – exploded off to one side and he fought with the controls as the Tempest slewed violently, the port wing dropping dangerously.

The whole aircraft was beginning to shudder and vibrate alarmingly and the engine was overheating badly. Mercifully, the flak died away behind him as he swept clear of the airfield, but he decided to stay low down for a few more seconds in case there were any other concealed anti-aircraft posts in his path.

As yet, he had no way of telling how badly the Tempest was hit. She was still responding to the controls, and for the time being that was enough. However, he knew that he dared not maintain full combat boost for long; five minutes was the maximum even under the best conditions, and in its damaged state there was a real danger that the aircraft would shake itself apart.

The sun was behind him and the Tempest's nose was pointed towards the west, so at least he was heading in the right direction, but his compass was smashed and he would have to rely on map-reading alone to get him home.

He climbed to eight thousand feet and throttled back, changing to 'S' gear and reducing to 2,500 rpm. The shuddering died away, although an occasional tremor continued to shake the aircraft. At least, he thought, she was still flying, and if the worst happened he now had sufficient height to bale out.

Carefully, checking off item by item, he took stock of his situation. His face was stinging badly, but when he removed his flying glove and made an exploratory probe with his fingers he found that there was very little blood, so his hurts must be only superficial. The worst discomfort came from the blast of freezing air that punched its way into the cockpit through the jagged hole in the canopy; the shell fragment, Yeoman thought with a sudden shiver of reaction, must have missed his head by inches.

In a sense he was grateful for the hole. A film of oil was spreading gradually over the canopy and windscreen, and as he flew on the hole became a window on the outside world. It was a highly dangerous situation in which he found himself, for with his vision impaired he would be easy prey for any prowling German fighters; the only alternative was to jettison the canopy, and that would mean freezing to death by slow degrees.

At least three vital instruments, the airspeed indicator, engine speed indicator and altimeter, were still intact, but most of the others were a confusion of shattered dials. Worst of all, his radio was completely dead, so there was no possibility of calling up Eindhoven – or any other Allied airfield, for that matter – to obtain a course to steer.

The minutes ticked by with agonizing slowness. Behind Yeoman, the rising sun disappeared behind a bank of cloud. The engine was still overheating, and every so often it missed a beat. As the crippled Tempest flew on, it trailed a thin ribbon of smoke across the sky.

In the embattled sky south of Bremen, Simon Wynne-Williams

had heard Yeoman's brief radio call but had been unable to answer it immediately, being fully occupied in a cut-and-thrust fight against two Focke-Wulfs. He managed to dispose of one with a well-aimed two-second burst and saw it go down trailing brilliant white flames, then looked for the other to find that it was disappearing into the distance. The reason, Wynne-Williams quickly discovered, was the presence of the other two Tempests of Red Section, which had come to his assistance.

Wynne-Williams radioed Phelan, who was Yeoman's deputy, and asked for permission to detach the three Tempests of Red Section to go to the Wing Commander's assistance. Phelan granted it readily and the three Tempests at once swung away towards the north-west in a shallow dive.

Wynne-Williams got his bearings and located the remains of the first Focke-Wulf destroyed by Yeoman; a pall of dense smoke drifted slowly across the fields from the blazing fragments. A couple of miles further on the shattered wreck of a second aircraft also burned fiercely; Wynne-Williams swept low over it, fearing the worst, then saw a black cross stamped on a shattered wing and knew that Yeoman had found another victim.

But where was Yeoman? Further radio calls brought no response; it was as though the sky had swallowed up the Wing Commander's Tempest completely. Wynne-Williams decided that there was no point in remaining in the dangerous vicinity of Bremen to carry out what might prove to be a fruitless search; if Yeoman had been hit but was still flying, he would be on his way home.

'All right, Red Section, let's get out of here. Steer 225 degrees and keep your eyes peeled.'

The three Tempests turned towards the south-west, following a homeward route towards the Dutch border and keeping well clear of Rheine airfield. Twenty miles further on, near Osterwick, a thread of smoke drawn across the sky led them to Yeoman's limping aircraft.

Yeoman glanced back through the oil-blurred canopy and his heart leaped into his throat when he saw the three aircraft bearing down on him. His hand tightened on the stick, ready to turn and face them. If this was to be his last fight, he was determined to make it a costly one for the enemy.

An indescribable surge of relief flooded through him when he saw that the aircraft were Tempests. They formed up alongside him and somehow their presence was like a heady tonic coursing through his veins, even though he knew deep down that his crippled fighter would almost certainly never reach Eindhoven.

Wynne-Williams, formating close to Yeoman's port wingtip, surveyed the other's aircraft with considerable alarm. The metal of the rear fuselage was riddled with jagged holes of varying sizes; it was a miracle that the control cables had not been sliced through. There were holes in the wings, too, and a big one in the cockpit canopy through which Wynne-Williams could see the pilot's head and shoulders. He was relieved when Yeoman looked across and waved reassuringly; his friend did not appear to be hurt, or at least not badly.

Suddenly, Wynne-Williams saw that Yeoman's Tempest was losing height, slowly but surely. It was already down to three thousand feet. Moreover, the trail of smoke from its exhaust stubs was growing thicker with every passing second.

The River Maas was ahead of them. Beyond it lay a strip of enemy-held territory, some ten miles across, and then safety. But ten miles was much, much too far.

Yeoman's labouring fighter struggled across the Maas, losing height quickly now. Wynne-Williams knew that it would never get clear of enemy territory now; he also knew that it was too low for Yeoman to have any chance of baling out. Urgently, he called up the other two Tempests.

'He's going down. Cover him – watch out for flak and small arms fire!'

The three Tempests went down almost to ground level, rocking their wings as they quartered the landscape, their pilots alert to any possible threat to Yeoman's crippled aircraft. The latter, gushing smoke now, was in a flat glide towards a long field by the side of a small river. Wynne-Williams followed it down, noting that Yeoman had jettisoned his cockpit canopy.

Hammering through Wynne-Williams' mind was the

thought that a belly-landing in a Tempest was the most dangerous thing in the world. The flaps had to be lowered half-way and the tail kept well down until the moment of impact, which occurred at about 170 mph. If the nose was allowed to drop, the huge scoop of the radiator would dig into the ground and the aircraft would immediately flip over on its back, trapping the pilot in the cockpit.

'Look out, flak!'

Red Three's shout echoed over the radio and Wynne-Williams immediately put his aircraft in a tight turn, first to the left and then to the right, and quickly located the enemy gun position. The Germans had converted a windmill into a flak tower, and from it a stream of fiery coals converged on Red Three, who was twisting frantically away from the danger.

The enemy fire crept round in an arc towards Wynne-Williams as the latter sped like a bullet across the mile or so of ground that separated him from the flak post. His thumb jabbed down on the gun button and he kept it there, seeing his shells churn up great fountains of mud near the windmill's base. A slight backward pressure on the control column, and the shells 'walked' up the side of the windmill in a trail of flying bricks to explode on the gun itself. Wynne-Williams had a glimpse of dark figures hurling themselves in terror from the parapet and then he was thundering overhead, turning back hard to where Yeoman had come down.

The Wing Commander's Tempest was a crumpled heap, lying two-thirds of the way into the field at the end of a long scar of churned-up earth. One wing had been torn off completely; the engine cowling was partly buried in the mud and the fuselage was broken aft of the cockpit.

Wynne-Williams roared low overhead, looking down. There was no sign of the pilot. But half a mile away, German soldiers in an extended line were running hard across the fields towards the wreck. The other Tempest pilots had seen them too, and without waiting for instructions they dived down to make a strafing run, unleashing a devastating fury of cannon fire at the enemy.

Wynne-Williams circled Yeoman's shattered aircraft,

quartering the area around it, reasoning that the pilot could not be far away. He spotted him suddenly, crouching in the shelter of a railway embankment. Yeoman waved as Wynne-Williams cruised slowly past, then gesticulated several times towards the wrecked Tempest.

His number two got his meaning almost at once. Every Tempest was fitted with demolition charges, so that the pilot could destroy the aircraft in the event of a forced landing in enemy territory, but it was clear that Yeoman had not been able to activate them for some reason – and the Wing Commander's aircraft was one of four in the Eindhoven Wing that had been fitted with a brand new type of 'Identification Friend or Foe' radio transponder which enabled a friendly controller not only to distinguish between Allied and enemy formations, but also to tell one Allied formation from another by means of coloured blips on his radar tube.

The equipment, Wynne-Williams knew, must not be allowed to fall intact into enemy hands. Bringing the Tempest round in a tight S-turn, a few feet above the ground, he lined up with Yeoman's aircraft and opened fire. The effect was instantaneous and dramatic. The impact of his incendiary shells produced a vivid flash, followed by an expanding ball of flame as what was left of the fuel in the wreck's tanks exploded.

He flew over the remains, making sure that the destruction was as complete as possible, then climbed to a thousand feet and looked around to get his bearings. He knew that the town he could see a few miles to the south was Venlo; a quick consultation with his map told him that the villages he could see immediately to north and south of the spot where Yeoman had crash-landed must be Venraij and Horst. The Allied lines were only ten miles away, with Eindhoven a similar distance beyond them.

The other Tempests were still snarling backwards and forwards at hedge-top height. The enemy troops had obviously gone to ground, and for good measure the Tempest pilots shot up a couple of trucks, which were now burning on a nearby road.

There was nothing more they could do to help Yeoman.

Wynne-Williams pointed the nose of his aircraft towards the west, called up the others and told them to go home. Behind them, in response to shouted commands, the German troops emerged from their cover and once more resumed their cautious advance towards the funeral pyre of Yeoman's Tempest.

6

Yeoman crouched in the narrow culvert and, despite his wet, miserable and muddy state, counted himself one of the luckiest men alive.

The culvert lay in the middle of a small wood and he suspected that it had long been forgotten. Once, the track through the wood must have been a well-used road, perhaps one trodden by local country folk taking their wares to market, but it was now badly overgrown and the stones of the culvert that channelled the waters of a stream under it were old and rough, covered by a deep layer of slimy moss.

Yeoman had stumbled on the little culvert quite by accident. The stream, along which he had waded in the hope of throwing any tracker dogs off the scent, had led him from the railway embankment in whose lee he had sheltered after running from his wrecked Tempest directly to the cover of the wood; plunging deeper into it, still following the stream, he had been surprised to find that the latter went underground. A rapid investigation had soon revealed the old culvert, running under the grass-grown mound of the track, its entrance and exit both screened by a tangle of thorns and roots.

Crawling inside, he had managed to find a slab of rock that rose just above water level and had squatted down on it, trying to make himself as comfortable as possible. He had spent all day in the wet half-darkness, clutching his service revolver, listening apprehensively for sounds of pursuit.

But there had been no pursuit – or at least none that came near his hiding-place. As the hours went by he had begun to relax a little, to take stock of his situation and to make plans.

He had bathed his cuts with icy water from the stream,

dabbed on his face with a clean handkerchief. Apart from a large bruise on his forehead where he had hit the Tempest's gunsight a glancing blow during the crash-landing, they were his only hurts. Shuddering, he recalled how close the fighter had come to turning over on its back during the long slide across the field; at one point it had stood almost on the end of its nose and he had hung there helplessly in his straps for what had seemed an age, staring at the earth, before the Tempest had slammed down on its belly again with a bone-jarring crunch.

The light began to fade steadily outside his man-made cave, and for the first time he felt a pang of hunger. He took a chocolate bar from the pocket of his battledress and ate half of it, savouring each morsel; there was no telling when he might eat again.

He was frozen to the marrow, but he had no intention of leaving his hiding place until nightfall. The temperature was dropping all the time, and he knew that his first and most urgent priority was to find drier, warmer shelter. He longed for a smoke, but convinced himself that it was too risky; the scent of tobacco could carry a very long way on frosty air. Instead, he sucked the stem of his unlit pipe and tried chewing a little tobacco, but this made him feel sick and he spat it out in disgust, washing out his mouth with a cupped handful of clear water from the stream.

At last, the glimmer of daylight that penetrated the culvert faded and then died altogether. Carefully, wincing with the pain of limbs that had been too long in a cramped position, he wormed his way through the thorns at the culvert's entrance and then knelt there in almost childlike wonder as he surveyed the transformed scene around him.

It must have been snowing all day, the big flakes falling calmly and unhurriedly as he crouched in his cavern. The snowfall lay two or three inches thick underfoot and the flakes were still floating down through the branches of the trees, brushing softly against Yeoman's face as he stood up and stretched gratefully. Somehow, it seemed warmer outside, out of the culvert's clammy darkness, and Yeoman knew that as long as it went on snowing his chances of evading capture would increase. Feeling his spirits rise, he ate a little more chocolate and then set off to walk through the wood, keeping a westerly direction with the help of a tiny, luminous escape compass which had been sewn into the lining of his battledress blouse.

His footfalls were noiseless on the carpet of snow. Although the flakes melted on his outer clothing and made it wet, he felt no undue discomfort; now that he was on the move his long woollen underclothing and thick sweater kept him reasonably warm, while his head was adequately covered by a woollen balaclava helmet which he always carried with him on operations.

As he walked, Yeoman found that he could see quite well. Probably because of the snow, the night – or rather the early evening, for his watch told him that it was only six o'clock – seemed to hold a kind of luminosity, and although he blundered into low-lying undergrowth on several occasions he had no difficulty in tracing a path among the trees, their trunks jutting up like tall sentinels amid the swirling whiteness.

As yet, Yeoman had not formed a clear idea about where he was going. It must, he surmised, be only a question of time until the enemy realized that his charred body did not lie in the remains of his Tempest, and resumed their search for him with the return of daylight; it was vital, therefore, that he covered as much ground as possible before daybreak, and since he knew that the British lines lay several miles to the west of his present position, it seemed logical to head in that direction. When daylight came, he would hole up again somewhere; beyond that, he had no other plan at present.

He walked slowly and cautiously, his .38 revolver gripped firmly in his right hand, alert for any strange sound around him; but total silence hung over the wood. Presently, the trees began to thin out, and when there were no longer any dark shapes in front of him he knew that he must be standing at the woodside. It was difficult to see anything now in the falling snow, but he thought that the ground sloped away quite sharply.

Well, he thought, I can't hang around here. There's only one way to go, and that's forward.

He took a single stride, and at that moment something cold and hard jabbed into the back of his neck. His mouth dropped open in astonishment as a voice whispered swiftly in his ear in perfect English:

'All right, old boy. Hold it there. This is a shotgun, and if you don't do exactly as I tell you I'll blow your head off. We'll take your peashooter.'

A hand reached out from the darkness and relieved Yeoman of his revolver. The pilot's mind was in total confusion. 'We', the man with the shotgun had said. That meant more than one. But who were they? Friends or enemies? In a strangled voice, flinching away slightly from the cold menace of the shotgun at his neck, he started to voice his questions, only to be cut short by a curt command from behind.

'Not now, old boy. Just do as I say, and everything'll be all right. Now start walking – not too fast, mind. Keep going a little to the left. That's it. There's a path here somewhere, leading down the hillside. We won't find it in this snow, of course, but if we follow the general direction we won't fall over the rocks and things.'

The fellow's almost conversational, Yeoman thought bemusedly, and did as he was told, urged on by the shotgun. Once or twice he toyed with the idea of making a break for it, although he knew he would not get very far. Besides, not daring to turn his head, he had no means of knowing how many men had taken him prisoner, or whether they were all armed. They had his revolver, he thought ruefully, as well as the shotgun.

They went on down the hillside. Several times, at a hissed command from the man with the shotgun, they stopped for a minute, and Yeoman guessed that his captors were listening intently. That, at least, was a good sign; if they were afraid of being detected by the Germans, the latter were obviously not friends of theirs. Nevertheless, being driven into the unknown at gunpoint like this was an unnerving experience, and he was thankful when, a few minutes later, they came to the village.

* * *

Vrouw Hetta van Oosten was preparing the evening meal, such as it was, and indulging in one of the daydreams that were becoming more and more frequent in these frugal times. She was dreaming of the day when, God willing, she would once more be reunited with her eldest son, Paul.

A merchant seaman, Paul had been in Java when, in 1942, the Japanese had swept across the Dutch East Indies. There had been a long period of heartbreak when she had been convinced that he was dead; then, only a few months ago, had come the news that he was in an internment camp.

She sighed deeply and looked down at the porridge she had been stirring over the fire. It was not much, but in these times when German-occupied Holland was starving it was enough to fill the bellies of herself and her younger son. And, she thought with a sudden smile, the bellies of those others who happened to pass her way from time to time. . . .

She glanced up at the photograph of her two sons, standing next to that of her dead husband on the mantelpiece. Her husband had been gone from her these ten years now, carried away swiftly and silently by a tumour on the brain, and in a way it was just as well. Far better that than slavery under the Germans.

Suddenly, above the crackling of the fire, she heard a new sound: a gentle tapping at the window. Startled, she turned away from the fire, listening. A moment later the sound came again, a little more insistently this time.

Quickly, Vrouw van Oosten turned down the lamp so that the room was lit only by the flickering fire, and crossed over to the door. Lifting the heavy curtain that covered it, she turned the key and opened the door an inch or two until it stuck against its safety chain. An urgent voice whispered from the darkness.

'Quickly, mother. It's me!'

'Henrik! Thank God! I thought something must have happened.'

She opened the door to admit her younger son and the two men who were with him, then quickly replaced the chain, turned the key in the lock again and re-adjusted the curtain.

Then, turning up the lamp once more, she scrutinized the man who was a stranger to her house.

'So,' she murmured, 'what have we here? Another flyer, by the look of it. Ah, your poor face! I shall tend to that in a moment. But first of all, you must have something to eat.'

She reached up and touched Yeoman's cheek lightly. The latter smiled, although he had not understood a word she had said, and watched her as she turned back to the bubbling pot on the fire. Then he looked at his unaccustomed surroundings, feeling the warmth of the fire seep through to his bones.

He was in a cottage kitchen, and for a moment he felt that he had been catapulted back in time a hundred years or more. The focal point of the room was the big open fireplace, with its built-in brick oven; two rocking chairs stood one on either side of it, facing each other. Around it, hanging on hooks, were pots and pans of various shapes and sizes, and a long shelf above it bore a row of pewter mugs and plates, gleaming dully in the mellow light. More plates and dishes were ranged on a dark wooden dresser that occupied an adjacent wall. In the centre of the room stood a roughly-hewn table, its spotless top scrubbed white, flanked by two wooden benches. A door in one corner led, Yeoman guessed, into another room that was doubtless reserved for special occasions, while a narrow staircase in the corner opposite ended at a trapdoor which presumably gave access to sleeping quarters.

Yeoman's appraisal of the kitchen took no more than a couple of seconds, after which his attention turned to the two men who had made him their prisoner. One of them, the younger of the two, had seated himself on one of the benches by the table; a bland, round-faced youth with fair hair and pink cheeks, he was gazing at Yeoman with a mixture of curiosity and admiration. Embarrassed, the pilot turned his eyes away and surveyed the other, who was standing with his back to the door, smiling at him.

The man was tall and dark-haired, with a lantern jaw, a long, straight nose and thin moustache. There was a livid scar running down one cheek, from his temple to the corner of his mouth. His smile did not reach his eyes, which were a pale, icy blue.

'Well, old boy,' the man said, in his cultured English, 'here we are. Time for some introductions, I think.'

He looked at the pilot questioningly. The latter noted that he still cradled the shotgun, and looked prepared to use it. Hastily, he told the man who he was, producing his identity disc and adding that he had been shot down that morning.

'Oh yes,' the man told him, 'we saw that. One of our friends told us that you'd legged it for the woods, too. Young Henrik here guessed where you'd hidden yourself; he knows the woods like the back of his hand. Thought it best to leave you where you were until nightfall and then make contact, just in case Jerry got to you first.'

Suddenly, the man gave a disarming grin, laid the shotgun to one side and stuck out his hand.

'Mike Chapman,' he said. 'Major, 1st Airborne Division. And before that, Second Battalion the Sherwood Foresters.' He pointed at the gun. 'Sorry about the ironmongery, but we have to be very careful, as I'm sure you will appreciate.'

Vrouw van Oosten interrupted the conversation briefly by setting bowls of steaming porridge on the table, together with some cheese and dark bread. She motioned to them to sit down and they fell to hungrily after first shedding their wet outer clothing, which she placed by the fire to dry.

Yeoman, his bowl half finished, swallowed a mouthful of hot porridge and looked at Chapman.

'First Airborne Division, you said. Were you at Arnhem?'

The other nodded. 'That's right. Went into the bag with all the other poor devils – those who were left, I mean. I managed to jump off a prisoner of war train just over the German border, somewhere near Venlo, and started walking north-west. Fell in with some friendly Dutch people and ended up here. Couldn't get any further, so decided to stay on and wait for the Allied advance to catch up with me. Quite a nice set-up, don't you think?'

Yeoman set down his spoon and stared at him.

'Surely,' he said, 'it must be possible to get across the enemy lines? Damn it, we can't just sit here and wait for something to happen! After all there are only two of us!'

Chapman chuckled. 'Two of us! My dear fellow, please forgive me if I correct you. Within a five-mile radius of this village there are forty-three Allied soldiers and airmen, some survivors of the Arnhem operation, others shot-down aircrew like yourself, all in hiding and waiting for a chance to get out!' He shook his head. 'No, old boy, it's impossible. We'd have to get across the Deurne Canal, and the German defences there are so tight that even a bat couldn't get through. The best thing for us is to stay underground and wait for the next Allied offensive. It can't be long now.'

Yeoman was far from convinced, but decided to keep his opinions to himself for the time being. Instead, he asked:

'Are there German troops in the village?'

'Oh yes, old boy,' Chapman assured him cheerfully, 'dozens of 'em. Or rather, there were until a couple of days ago, when there was a hell of a commotion and they all went off somewhere. All but a few, that is.'

He popped a piece of cheese into his mouth and said, chewing:

'As a matter of fact, there are a couple of German officers billeted in the house next door. They sometimes pop in for a cup of coffee. It's their own coffee, of course. They generously let Vrouw van Oosten have a packet from time to time. Nice of 'em, what?'

Yeoman stared at him in amazement. 'Good God!' he spluttered. 'Do you mean to tell me that enemy officers actually come here, to this house, while you are in it?'

'Of course they do, old chap,' smiled Chapman. 'But then, I'm in hiding for most of the time, so I don't actually see 'em face to face. Anyway, they're very obliging fellows – if they do turn up for coffee, it's always at the same time. No chance of being taken by surprise, or anything like that.'

'But – don't they ever carry out house searches?' the pilot wanted to know. Chapman looked faintly astonished.

'Good Lord, no! The Dutch folk around here are noted for being very co-operative. The Germans trust 'em. After all, just a few miles further east and these people would have been Germans themselves, what?' He laughed hugely, and despite his fears Yeoman saw an amusing irony in the whole situation.

He was sitting in the middle of an incredible escape network – and one that functioned, moreover, right under the noses of the unsuspecting enemy.

Nevertheless, he felt uneasy. The Dutch people who ran the escape line were taking an appalling risk, and if they were discovered by the Germans, they would receive no mercy. Yet when he glanced at the rosy faces of Vrouw van Oosten and her son, Henrik, he saw no trace of anxiety there. To them, helping Allied soldiers and airmen was a simple duty, and one they would not have shirked for all the rewards in the world. Yeoman felt very humble.

He finished the last of his bread and cheese, took a drink of hot milk and stretched out his hands towards the fire, sighing contentedly. As an afterthought, he pulled out his pipe and asked if he might smoke.

Chapman translated his request to Vrouw van Oosten, then looked at Yeoman and nodded.

'She says it'll be all right, old boy – but sit by the fire, if you don't mind, so that your smoke goes up the chimney. Then if anyone comes in unexpectedly, the house won't be smelling of English tobacco!'

While the pilot sat by the fire and smoked, the housewife bathed his face tenderly and applied some sort of ointment to the cuts. When she finished her task she patted him on the shoulder, then busied herself with clearing away the dishes. Yeoman stared into the fire and went on puffing at his pipe, his eyelids drooping drowsily. He was suddenly aware of how tired he felt; his head throbbed and he ached all over as the strain and reaction of the day's events finally caught up with him.

His chin fell on his chest and he jerked awake with a start, looking round and wondering for a moment where he was. His pipe, still held tightly in his hand, had gone out. Chapman was sitting in the chair opposite, looking at him sympathetically.

'You look absolutely done in, old chap,' he said. 'You'd better get off to bed – the others went ages ago. I've organized some blankets and things for you.'

He picked up Yeoman's battledress blouse from the clothes-horse where it had been drying in front of the dying fire and threw it across to him.

'Better take this with you. Remove the evidence, just in case, eh?'

He led the pilot up the staircase and through the trapdoor into a low attic. It had been converted into two small bedrooms, and Chapman explained in a whisper that Henrik slept in one of them while his mother slept downstairs to make room for her 'guests'.

By the light of the lamp, Chapman showed Yeoman the makeshift bed he had made in one corner.

'There you are, old boy,' he said. 'It's all yours. I suggest you sleep with your clothes on; it can get pretty cold up here. And try not to snore too loudly. Remember the Jerries next door!'

Yeoman looked at the bed and thought that he had never seen anything so inviting. Pulling off his boots, he burrowed his way into the blankets and was asleep in seconds.

At five-thirty the following morning, her accustomed time, winter and summer alike, Vrouw van Oosten awoke and got quickly out of bed, pulling a thick, warm shawl over her shoulders. She went into the kitchen and made the fire, dressing herself in its glow, then unlocked the door and peered out into the freezing darkness of the winter morning. It had stopped snowing, but now a raw, chill fog clung to the land.

Smiling to herself, she lifted down the laurel wreath that hung from a nail on the door – an age-old village custom that probably went back to pagan times – and took it into the warmth of the kitchen. Tied to the bottom of the wreath was a faded strand of red ribbon; she carefully removed it and tied a new strip of blue ribbon in its place before replacing the wreath on the door. When the village postman came round later he would see the blue ribbon, wink at her in knowing silence, and spread the word. And before the morning was out, various callers would knock on her door, bringing morsels of food and other comforts for Vrouw van Oosten's extra guest. . . .

As she hung the wreath back on its nail she paused for a moment in the doorway, her head cocked on one side, listening. From somewhere far away there came a dull rumble, as of distant thunder, deadened by the blanket of fog and almost inaudible.

Well, she thought, whatever it was, it was no threat to her or the others in her house. She shrugged her shoulders and went inside.

7

Under cover of the fog, the German troops had been moving into their forward assembly areas for many hours. Now, in the chill early hours of Saturday, 16 December 1944, a comparative silence reigned over the Ardennes as though the mountains and wooded hillsides themselves were waiting expectantly for the holocaust that was to come.

Then, at 0530, the whole length of the Ardennes front was split by vivid flame as two thousand German guns opened up simultaneously between Monschau and Echternach, hurling a devastating weight of shellfire into the forward outposts of the unsuspecting Americans. For two hours the onslaught went on, and in its wake the panzers and the mechanized infantry moved relentlessly forward to the attack.

The German commanders knew the terrain in the Ardennes well. They had advanced across it during the Blitzkrieg of May 1940 and had retreated through it again four years later. They knew its narrow, twisting roads and the difficulties and dangers that were certain to be experienced in negotiating them in the middle of winter and in the bad weather conditions which were essential to the success of the operation. To get the guns of the artillery and flak units as well as the pontoons of the bridging engineers round the sharp hairpin bends, the guns and trailers had to be disconnected and then dragged round the corners one at a time by a winch mechanism. In many ways, it was a labour comparable to Hannibal's passage through the Alps – and the miracle was that, like Hannibal's venture, it succeeded.

The initial German onslaught, smashing like a hammer blow out of the fog and aided by the artillery barrage, which had cut communications, threw the weak and thinly-scattered American defences into complete confusion. Some isolated outposts had time to organize themselves and put up a fierce resistance before they were overwhelmed, and their gallant sacrifice, by slowing down the enemy's timetable, was to play a significant part in the final outcome of the Ardennes battle.

For the time being, however, it seemed that nothing could stop the German thrust. By 19 December, the panzer spearheads had driven nearly sixty miles into Belgium, overrunning towns and villages whose inhabitants had so recently celebrated their liberation. It was a phenomenal success, causing almost total disarray in the Allied command structure, and as the Panzer divisions plunged on wild hopes began to grow in the hearts of even the most sceptical of the German soldiers.

'We have been on our way through Belgium without a break,' wrote one young Panzer Grenadier to his wife. 'No rest or sleep at all. The main thing is that the Americans are on the run. We cleared an enemy supply dump . . . everybody took only the things he wanted most. I took only chocolate. I have all my pockets full of it. I eat chocolate all the time, in order to sweeten somewhat this wretched life . . . Don't worry about me. The worst is behind me. Now this is just a hunt.'

And another wrote fervently: 'This time we are a thousand times better off than you at home. You cannot imagine what glorious hours and days we are experiencing now. It looks as if the Americans cannot withstand our important push. Today we overtook a fleeing column and finished it. We overtook it by taking a back road through the woods to the retreat lane of the American vehicles; then, just like on manoeuvres, we pulled up along the road with sixty Panthers. And then came the endless convoy driving in two columns, side by side, hub on hub, filled to the brim with soldiers. And then a concentrated fire from sixty guns and one hundred and twenty machine-guns. It was a glorious bloodbath, vengeance for our destroyed homeland. Our soldiers still have the old zip. Always advancing and smashing everything. The snow must turn red with American blood. Victory was never as close as it is now. . . .'

By nightfall on 19 December, three days after the start of the offensive, the thrusting German columns had succeeded in isolating and taking prisoner nine thousand American troops in the Schnee Eifel area. It was the worst reverse suffered on the continent of Europe by the United States Army in this war and the previous one.

Nevertheless, many factors combined in holding up the German advance and the prospects of a massive breakthrough on the Meuse. One key factor in the German plan had been to use some two thousand paratroops, disguised as American soldiers, to capture the Meuse bridges and several vital fuel dumps, from whose stocks the speeding panzers were to replenish; but although the paratroops managed to sow a good deal of confusion in the beginning, the Americans quickly grasped what was happening and launched a major round-up operation. Any Germans who were caught masquerading as Americans were summarily executed.

The biggest stumbling block to the success of the German offensive, however, was the town of Bastogne, which lay directly in the path of the assault's left flank. The Germans fully realized the importance of Bastogne in their drive towards the Meuse; at a briefing several days before the start of the offensive, General von Luttwitz, commanding 47th Panzer Corps, had told his subordinate commanders:

'Bastogne must be taken eventually from the rear. If it is not taken it will always remain an ulcer on our lines of communication and for this reason will contain too many of our forces. Therefore, first clear out Bastogne and then carry on.'

But it was not to prove as simple as that. The Americans, recognizing the serious threat to Bastogne, diverted the crack 101st Airborne Division to reinforce the units that were already there. For several days, exhausted, hungry and half frozen, suffering appalling casualties, they were to hold grimly on to Bastogne in the teeth of relentless German attacks from three points of the compass.

Still the fog persisted, effectively keeping the air forces of both sides glued to the ground. And on the night of Wednesday, 20 December, the thermometer fell dramatically and the snow once more began to fall, covering the bodies of the dead that lay between the opposing lines. The ground froze hard, and the defenders of Bastogne knew that the panzers – which had hitherto been restricted to the roads because of muddy conditions – would soon be rolling across the snowy plain to smash through the perimeter, while on the other side of the line the Germans were beginning to look apprehensively at a sky that was starting to show signs of clearing.

When the sky cleared the Allied fighter-bombers would come, dealing out death and destruction on a scale approaching that of the Falaise battle several months earlier; and the German armour was still a long way short of its primary objective, the River Meuse. . . .

'I'm sorry, Mike,' Yeoman said, his face set and determined, 'but I've made my mind up. I'm going to make a break for it tonight. I've been here for four days, and it's too long, especially in view of the news.'

Thanks to a clandestine radio set operated by a neighbour, they were all aware of the great German push in the Ardennes. Yeoman and Chapman had both been stunned by the news, for neither had believed that the enemy still had sufficient resources in the west to mount such an undertaking.

'Well, old boy,' Chapman told him, 'I think you're being a damn fool, if you don't mind my saying so. But I can see that nothing I can say will shake you. What are you planning to do?'

Yeoman pondered for a moment, then said: 'I've thought it out pretty carefully. I can't get across the Deurne Canal, because all the crossing points have been blown and I'm no swimmer, especially in this weather. So I'm going to try and by-pass it. Look, here's what I mean.'

He fished in his pocket and withdrew a scrap of paper on which he had drawn a sketch map, partly from memory and partly with the help of Henrik. He pointed at it with the stem of his pipe.

'Here we are, look, at Venraij. Now then, the Deurne Canal is only four miles away to the west as the crow flies, but as we both agree there is very little prospect of getting across it. Instead, I plan to strike out northwards, following the railway line that leads to Nijmegen. I reckon that if I keep walking in this direction, I'll be able to reach the salient our people have pushed through into the Nijmegen area and slip through into friendly territory somewhere near Grave, just here. I calculate that about fifteen miles of walking should do it, and if I allow myself a mile an hour across country then I should cover the distance in two nights, lying up during the daytime. Now, what do you think?'

Chapman looked dubiously at him. 'I think you're bloody mad,' he said. 'Fifteen miles through an area crawling with Jerries might just as well be fifteen hundred. Still, since you're quite obviously in a determined mood, I'm prepared to give you all the help I can.'

He pursed his lips thoughtfully, then turned and spoke in Dutch to Henrik. The young man listened gravely, then nodded.

'Henrik has agreed to go with you as far as Boxmeer,' Chapman told the pilot. The latter opened his mouth to protest, but was cut short by a wave of the army officer's hand.

'No buts, old boy. Henrik will take you to Boxmeer, which is about seven or eight miles from here. We've a contact there, you see, who is hiding some of our chaps. He'll put you up for the night and set you on your way again the next day. Now, let's get down to the finer details.'

For the next couple of hours the men went over Yeoman's plan in detail. Vrouw van Oosten gave Yeoman a disapproving look when she learned of his intentions, but nevertheless she made up a bundle of food from her meagre supply and pressed it on him. She also gave him a cloth cap and an overcoat which had once belonged to her husband; the coat was ragged, but it would serve as extra protection against the winter weather, and Yeoman was glad of it.

The pilot and Henrik waited until it was ten o'clock, then slipped quietly out of the house after making their whispered farewells. Chapman gripped Yeoman's hand tightly and said with a trace of wistfulness in his voice:

'Goodbye, old chap. Now that you're leaving, I wish I were coming with you. But I'd better stay here, I suppose, and make sure the others are organized when the time comes.'

Yeoman gripped the other's shoulder. 'So long, Mike. I'll make sure our people know all about you, when I get back. It won't be long before you're out of here. In the meantime, keep your head down.'

The two men did not look back as they moved stealthily away from the house into the foggy darkness. Yeoman followed Henrik blindly, trusting the young man implicitly as he led him up dark alleys and along paths that wound their way through gardens. Once, they froze into immobility as something moved in the swirling vapour ahead of them; but it was only a dog, and with a low growl it scurried away into the night.

The thin layer of snow that covered the ground was frozen hard, and their feet made scarcely any impression as they walked on. Henrik, who knew exactly where he was, kept up a fast pace, and despite the intense cold Yeoman was soon perspiring. It was a relief when, after moving across country for some two miles, they reached the railway line and began to walk along it.

Yeoman knew that trains no longer moved along this stretch of track, for the twenty-five miles of line between Venlo and Nijmegen had long since been blasted out of recognition by Allied bombs and the Germans had given up their attempts at repairing it. In places, the two men found the going very hard, for they were compelled to skirt or clamber over great mounds of frozen earth that still surrounded old bomb craters. On two occasions, they were forced to clamber up the embankment and move in open country for a while, for the line was completely blocked for hundred of yards where Allied fighter-bombers had destroyed rolling stock.

They reached the outskirts of Boxmeer at four o'clock in the morning, and Henrik made the pilot understand that they now had to move with extreme caution, for there were many Germans in the village. Yet, thankfully, there was not a soul in sight as they crept through the cobbled streets, moving silently from wall to sheltering wall like wraiths in the all-embracing fog; not a sound stirred the stillness except the rasp of their own breathing and the beating of their adrenalin-boosted hearts.

They turned a corner and Henrik stopped suddenly, laying a hand on Yeoman's arm and pointing. On the other side of a little square, just visible in the murk, was a church, and the pilot gathered that one of the houses close to it was their destination.

They sidled round the edge of the square and climbed a low wall at the far side, jumping down into a graveyard. Henrik paused for a moment to get his bearings, then led the pilot past a clump of bushes to a path that meandered through the tombstones, ending at a lych-gate. They passed through the latter, wincing as the metal hinges creaked alarmingly, climbed another wall on the other side of a narrow alley, and at last found themselves in the back yard of a house.

Yeoman almost fell over Henrik as the Dutchman bent down suddenly, groping for something in the darkness. A moment later, after some effort, a trapdoor swung open and Henrik indicated that the pilot was to climb down through it. Yeoman did so, lowering himself carefully over the edge and moving his feet about experimentally until they encountered the rungs of a ladder. He scrambled quickly down, followed by Henrik, who closed the trapdoor over their heads, and stood motionless in the inky blackness, wondering what was coming next.

He heard the rattle of matches, then blinked as a sudden flare of light split the darkness. Shielding the flame in his cupped hand, the Dutchman went over to an oil lamp that was hanging from the ceiling and lit it. Then he reached out and pulled a thin, rusty chain that disappeared into a hole in the wall. Distantly, a bell tinkled.

In the lamp's glow, Yeoman saw that they were standing in a fairly large cellar. From its smell, he guessed that it had once been used for storing malt, although it was now empty. He looked at Henrik and raised a questioning eyebrow, but the Dutchman just smiled and motioned with his thumb towards a heavy wooden door that was let into one of the cellar walls at the head of a small flight of worn steps.

Several minutes passed, and then the pilot tensed as he heard soft footfalls somewhere beyond the closed door. Gently, an unseen hand rapped on it; two knocks, then three, then two more. Crossing to the door, Henrik answered with a different code.

Instantly, there was the sound of heavy bolts being drawn, and the door swung open to admit a gigantic figure of a man. He wore corduroy trousers and a long-sleeved vest under which huge muscles bulged, and in one great ham of a fist he carried a Sten sub-machine-gun. His face, under a stubble of closely-cropped yellow hair, was amiable, and it split into a huge grin as he came down the cellar steps towards Henrik.

The two Dutchmen held a brief and rapid conversation, and then the giant turned to Yeoman and said in surprisingly good English:

'Welcome to my home, Wing Commander. My young friend Henrik tells me that you are planning to cross the front line. It is a dangerous thing to try and do. There are many German positions, many minefields. But come, we will talk in more comfortable surroundings.'

He led the way out of the cellar up a long flight of stone steps that ended in a kitchen. They passed straight through it, walked along a short passage and entered a small oak-panelled room. The giant ushered them inside, then, setting down the lantern he had brought from the cellar with him, he picked up some wood from the hearth and tossed it on the embers of the fire. Sparks showered up the chimney and tiny flames began to lick at the kindling.

The giant straightened up again, smiling.

'Please sit down.' His voice was like the muted rumbling of a volcano. 'You must be cold after your long walk. Let me offer you something to drink. Brandy, perhaps?'

Yeoman, in fact, had not realized how cold he was until he entered the warm room and felt his face and hands begin to tingle uncomfortably. He accepted the drink gratefully, looking round the room with his habitual curiosity as he sipped it. Apart from the leather settee on which Yeoman and Henrik now sat, and a big easy chair into which the giant eased his huge body, the furniture consisted solely of bookshelves. They lined every wall, leaving room only for a great painting of the Madonna and Child that hung over the fireplace. Beneath the picture, a flame burned in a holder of red glass.

Yeoman gestured towards the bookshelves. 'May I?' he asked.

The giant smiled and nodded. 'By all means, although I fear you will find them of little interest.'

The pilot roamed around the room, inspecting the book titles closely in the lamplight. He discovered that most of the books were religious works in many different languages, some of them very old.

'The tools of my trade,' smiled the giant. 'Or rather they used to be. You see, I was once a Roman Catholic priest. I was, shall we say, compelled to resign. There was some trouble over a woman. It was all a very long time ago.'

'What do you do now?' Yeoman asked, attempting to avert a conversation which, he felt, might prove embarrassing to the ex-priest. The smile faded from the latter's face and a sudden transformation came over him, as though he had switched from one personality to another. His eyes became hooded, and Yeoman all at once had the impression that his great body, as well as possessing enormous strength, could move with the speed of a striking cobra.

'I kill Germans,' the former priest said in a quiet, matter-of-fact voice. Yeoman felt his scalp crawl.

The giant questioned him about his intentions, and Yeoman showed him the sketch map he had made. The ex-priest gave a grunt, went over to one of the bookshelves and took down a large-scale map of the area, which he unfolded and spread out on the floor under the lamplight. He knelt beside it, and gestured to Yeoman to do the same. Then, as thoroughly as a military commander at a briefing, he outlined the course of action the pilot would have to take if he was to have any hope of getting across the front line to safety.

Yeoman learned that over the past few days, the German forces still in the narrow salient west of the River Maas had been considerably reinforced. The most likely explanation, he felt, was that their purpose was to thwart any sudden attack by the British Second Army in an attempt to take some of the pressure off the Americans further to the south, in Belgium. Whatever the reason, the whole of the Deurne Canal line was now more strongly fortified than ever before; the only possible way through it was by way of the wooded area to the south of Nijmegen.

There, a narrow tributary of the Maas joined that river with the canal, flowing through the town of Grave. On the other side of the tributary – which, the ex-priest said, the pilot should be able to negotiate – lay Allied territory. The snag was that the whole area was stiff with minefields and pillboxes, and even if he got through them, Yeoman would have to cross a mile and a half of no man's land before he reached safety. And, the ex-priest warned him, the ground was covered with snow; if the fog cleared, a solitary person trying to cross it, by day or night, would be easily seen by the enemy outposts and picked off.

The sound of gentle snoring interrupted their conversation. They both turned, startled, and laughed to see that Henrik had stretched himself out on the settee and was now fast asleep.

'That seems like an excellent idea,' Yeoman said. 'I'm feeling pretty tired myself, and I'd completely forgotten that we had dragged you out of your bed.'

'You can sleep here, in front of the fire,' the ex-priest told him. 'I will bring some blankets, and a pillow.' He heaped some more wood on the fire, then said:

'Rest for as long as you like. My housekeeper comes in before noon, but she is completely loyal and will not trouble you. Henrik, I think, will be gone by the time you wake. It will be noticed if he is absent from Venraij for too long, and that would not be a good thing.'

'Well,' the pilot said, 'I hope I'm awake to see him off. I owe him a great deal.'

In fact, the pilot woke much sooner than he had expected. Not long after daybreak, the thunder of massed aero-engines dragged him from his sleep.

Henrik was awake too, and after hesitating for a moment he risked a cautious peep through the heavy curtains that covered the room's solitary window. An instant later, he gave a gasp of astonishment and stepped aside to let Yeoman look out too.

The morning was brilliantly clear. There was no trace of the fog that had clung obstinately to the earth during the preceding days, and the snow on the roof-tops sparkled brightly in the rising sun.

The sun also caught the broad streaks of hundreds of vapour

trails, turning them a rosy pink. As Yeoman watched in fascination the tiny metallic dots that were the great heavy bombers curved slowly towards the south-east, heading for the busy marshalling yards and the supply depots of the Ruhr that were feeding and sustaining the German offensive in the Ardennes.

The enemy's last ally, the weather, had deserted him at last, and now the Allied air commanders had turned the tigers loose. As he watched that great phalanx of Flying Fortresses spearing into Germany, Yeoman knew that the enemy's last great push had been doomed to failure even before it had begun.

8

Saturday, 23 December, marked the turning point of the Ardennes battle. As the rays of the rising sun lit up dazzling white fields of fresh snow, airfields stretching in a great arc from England to Holland echoed to the thunder of engines as wave after wave of aircraft – transports, bombers, fighter-bombers and escort fighters – took off on their first mission for days.

In Bastogne, the haggard defenders greeted the brilliant dawn with apprehension. They had been bombed during the night and, their supplies of food and ammunition all but exhausted, they knew that this day might be their last. All that morning, as they managed to beat off enemy attacks around the perimeter, they waited for the big German onslaught which they knew they could not possibly withstand.

Instead, winging out of the western sky, came a huge armada of C-47 transport planes, with a screen of Lockheed Lightning fighters weaving protectively overhead. At a height of only a few hundred feet the transports flew straight and level towards their dropping zones, braving the intense flak that rose to meet them from the German positions. Some were hit and plunged helplessly to earth; the others forged on and their vital cargoes spilled from their bellies to float down under multi-coloured parachutes.

As each wave of transports turned for home, its mission completed, its escorting fighters swept down to strafe the enemy positions with rockets, fragmentation bombs and napalm, completing their attacks with machine-gun fire. The German troops cringed in their foxholes or under whatever cover they could find and cursed in terror; Hermann Goering, the Luftwaffe C-in-C, had promised them the support of two thousand aircraft as soon as the weather improved, but on this Saturday morning it was the Allied fighter-bombers – the hated and feared 'Jabos', as the Germans had nicknamed them – which ruled the air over Bastogne and, indeed, over the whole of the Ardennes.

It was not so further to the north, where both the Luftwaffe and the RAF's 2nd Tactical Air Force took advantage of the unexpected clear weather to resume intensive air operations. From first light onwards, the Focke-Wulfs and Messerschmitts of Joachim Richter's Jagdgeschwader 66 and two other wings carried out large-scale offensive patrols over Holland, seeking to catch and destroy the British fighter-bombers which were once more harassing the German ground forces in the area to the north of Nijmegen. On the first sortie of the day, Richter had an unexpected stroke of luck when, leading twenty FW 190s, he encountered a dozen Typhoons on their way home from a ground attack mission; in a fierce ten-minute battle his pilots destroyed six of them, he himself claiming one.

The Tempests of the Eindhoven Wing were not involved in the air fighting over Holland on this occasion. Because of their longer range, they were detailed to assist the Americans by operating in sections of four over the northern fringe of the Ardennes battle area. It was a task that was to bring an unexpected success to No. 505 Squadron.

At 1030 on the morning of 23 December, Tim Phelan – who was commanding the Wing in Yeoman's absence – was leading a section of Tempests consisting of Simon Wynne-Williams and two Sergeant Pilots named West and Renfrew; the four Tempests flew over the snow-shrouded, hilly countryside at four thousand feet, keeping above the enemy's light flak, and entered their patrol area a few miles south-east of Verviers. High above them, the cold blue sky was criss-crossed with the vapour trails of American heavy bombers, en route to their objectives inside Germany. While West and Renfrew kept a continual lookout behind, above and to either quarter, Phelan and Wynne-Williams searched the featureless snowscape for signs of enemy movement and for Luftwaffe fighter-bombers.

They also had to keep a close eye on the section's navigation, for they had been assigned a clearly-defined patrol sector and to stray out of it was to risk being fired on by American anti-aircraft guns or fighters.

Wynne-Williams, intent on peering at the ground – a task that made his eyes ache – suddenly realized that the last time he had flown in this area was four and a half years ago. German armoured columns had been thrusting through the Ardennes then, too, and the Hurricanes of No. 505 Squadron had formed part of the tiny RAF fighter force that had battled alongside the French and the Belgians against the might of the Luftwaffe. Over there, a few miles to the south, was Luxembourg, over which Jim Callender – an American serving with the RAF, who had since transferred to the USAAF – and George Yeoman had taken on a formation of Messerschmitts on that very first day of the German offensive in the west. Wynne-Williams had been shot down during that engagement, but after several adventures had succeeded in making his way across the River Meuse to friendly territory. He had fought on with his squadron until that terrible day, three months later, when he had fallen like a human torch from the cockpit of his blazing fighter over southern England.

The thought flashed through his mind that George Yeoman might be walking home at that very moment. A dark cloud had hung over Eindhoven since the Wing Commander had been lost in enemy territory a week earlier; there had been no news of him since, but everyone hoped that he was safe and that he had somehow evaded capture. If he could hole up somewhere, Wynne-Williams thought, he could maybe sit tight and wait until the army arrived.

He looked over to the right, towards Malmedy, and frowned, narrowing his eyes. Two thin black lines, like parallel railway tracks, were etched on the snow, some distance apart and a few miles away.

The sight puzzled him; if they had been railway lines, or some other feature, they would surely follow the contours of the countryside. These pencil-thin slashes looked out of place and unnatural.

Suddenly, it dawned on him. He pressed the R/T button and snapped out a warning.

'Smoke trails, three o'clock low!'

He could see that the trails were moving now, and could make out a black dot at the head of each one. It took Phelan only a second or two to locate them and realize what they were: jet-propelled Me 262s, their turbines leaving long trails of unburnt fuel that betrayed their position.

Phelan hesitated for a moment, watching the 262s carefully and making some quick mental calculations. If the jets maintained their present course they would cross the Tempests' noses at a range of perhaps two miles. But the enemy fighters were travelling very fast, and if they altered their heading even slightly the Tempests would have little chance of catching them.

Phelan ordered the section up to six thousand feet, keeping an eye on the jets all the time. The extra height would give them a vital margin of speed.

The 262s were closing the range fast. It was now or never.

'Three and Four, stay upstairs and cover us. Come on, Simon, let's go and get 'em!'

The two Tempests went into a long, shallow dive at full power, Phelan going after the left-hand 262 and Wynne-Williams the right-hand one. There was about half a mile between the jets. Wynne-Williams could see clearly now that what had originally appeared to be twin dark smoke trails were really four, two streaming in the wake of each jet. As the gap closed, more details of the enemy aircraft themselves became visible: the slender, shark-like fuselages, the swept-back wings.

The two Tempests were doing close on 500 mph now, and yet they were only just managing to overhaul the 262s. Wynne-Williams found himself holding his breath as the dark silhouette of his target crept inside the luminous diamonds of his reflector sight. His thumb caressed the gun button. Just a few more seconds . . .

The smoke trails from the 262's turbines suddenly became denser. Wynne-Williams swore and his thumb jabbed down on the button. The Tempest shuddered violently with the recoil as its four cannon pumped shells towards the enemy jet.

Almost beside himself with frustration and fury, Wynne-Williams saw his tracer fall away below the 262. The range was too great, and was increasing with every passing moment as the enemy pilot turned on every ounce of power. Out of the corner of his eye, the pilot saw that the second 262 was also speeding hell-for-leather for the German border.

'Stay with them! Three and Four, stay with us and watch our tails!'

Wynne-Williams heard one of the other Tempest pilots acknowledge Phelan's command and concentrated on the jet fighter ahead of him, which was still drawing away. Flak came slamming up at them from some unseen source, but the Tempests' phenomenal speed had caused the gunners to misjudge their deflection and the salvoes burst harmlessly behind.

Suddenly, Wynne-Williams felt a surge of elation as he saw the 262's smoke trails grow thinner, first behind one turbine and then the other. Almost immediately, the distance between the two aircraft began to close again. He realized at once what must have happened: the enemy pilot, returning home from his sortie and already low on fuel, had gambled that a last despairing burst of power would be enough to take him clear of the pursuing fighter. It was his misfortune that the pursuer was a Tempest, the fastest Allied fighter of all.

The chase continued at dizzying speed over the undulating snow-covered hillsides. Wynne-Williams found himself holding his breath as the black arrowhead-like silhouette of the 262 grew bigger in his sights. His own engine was beginning to overheat, and he knew that he could not keep up this pace for much longer.

The 262 seemed to hang poised between the luminous diamonds of the gunsight. Wynne-Williams stabbed his thumb down on the gun-button and held it there for two seconds.

It was a straightforward no-deflection shot, for the enemy pilot had made no attempt to take evasive action, and the effect was dramatic. There was a vivid flash on the 262's starboard turbine and instantly a long river of white flame streamed back, dying away a moment later to be replaced by dense smoke.

The jet fighter slewed violently to the left and started to roll. At that moment, its cockpit canopy flew off and a dark bundle shot out into the slipstream. Startled, Wynne-Williams saw it tumble away below. Later, he learned that he had become one of the first Allied pilots to witness an ejection seat in operation; but on this occasion the 262 had been too low and the unfortunate pilot had not had time to release himself from the seat and operate his parachute.

The 262, rolling helplessly now and coughing smoke and flames, continued its trajectory for a few hundred yards and then plunged into the trees with a terrific explosion.

Wynne-Williams roared over the billowing smoke cloud and pulled up in a climbing turn, levelling out at five thousand feet and throttling back his overworked engine, looking round for the others. A moment later, Phelan's Tempest slipped into position alongside, and the radio crackled into life.

'Nice work, Simon!'

Phelan, too, had got his 262. Wynne-Williams wondered if they had set up a new record: shooting down one of these speedy jets was a considerable feat in itself, but he had never before heard of a pair of them being destroyed in a single sortie. They would have to check up on that, when they got home.

'Did you pinpoint that flak, earlier on?' Phelan asked. Wynne-Williams told him that it had come from a spot close to the main road that led from Eupen to Malmédy, about two miles north of the latter town.

'Okay, then, let's take a look. It might be something important.'

The four Tempests flew along the line of the Warche River until they sighted Malmédy, then turned right, the pilots quartering the ground like hawks. Suddenly, anti-aircraft fire came up thick and fast, exploding all around them, and they quickly sheered off out of the danger zone.

'Christ, that was bloody close!' Phelan said. 'Did you get that?'

'Coming from the edge of that long wood,' Wynne-Williams

said, as they turned. 'Coming round into our nine o'clock, now.'

'Roger, I've got it. Good God, look at that lot!'

They spotted the gun positions and the enemy convoy at the same moment. The trucks, jammed bumper to bumper, stretched back for miles along the road; they had been cleverly camouflaged with light-coloured tarpaulins so that they would blend in with the snowy background.

'Do not attack,' Phelan ordered. 'I repeat, do not attack.'

It was a wise decision; Wynne-Williams knew that the enemy convoy would be stiff with flak, and a low-level attack on it by only four aircraft would be tantamount to suicide.

Instead, he climbed several thousand feet, to extend the range of his radio transmission, and called up Group Central Control, telling the controller what he had seen. The controller acknowledged, paused briefly, then said:

'Two squadrons of Typhoons have just taken off from Evere; I have told them to divert to your sector. Can you stay there for a while to guide them in?'

Phelan radioed that they had sufficient fuel to permit a further twenty minutes in their patrol sector.

'But tell the Tiffie boys to get a move on,' he added, 'and see if you can whistle up some Spitfires for top cover. If the Jerries see us stooging around for any length of time, they're bound to call up their fighter boys. It could get unhealthy.'

After a few minutes, the Typhoon leader came up over the R/T:

'Ramrod from Badger Leader. Understand from GCC you have some trade for us. Instructions, please.'

'Badger Leader from Ramrod. Rendezvous south-east of Verviers at eight thousand and I'll lead you in.'

The Typhoons soon came up over the northern horizon, flying in two boxes of twelve aircraft. The four Tempests jockeyed into position ahead of them and Phelan led them unerringly to the target. While the Tempests circled watchfully overhead, the Typhoons dived through a storm of anti-aircraft fire and let fly with rockets and cannon, one after the other. Looking down, Wynne-Williams thought how beautifully practised and organized they were; while a handful of Typhoons broke away and dived down to neutralize the flak batteries, the others began systematically to work over the enemy convoy, which was soon blazing from end to end.

The fighter-bombers were still at their work of destruction when the four Tempests turned for home, low on fuel. As they flew northwards, they passed a large formation of Spitfires, heading for the scene of the action. Half a dozen of the Spits broke formation and swept towards the Tempests to check on their identity, then waggled their wings and flew off, their pilots satisfied. The Tempests returned to base without incident and the pilots went off to make their intelligence reports, West and Renfrew grumbling somewhat because they had not had a chance to fire their guns.

They need not have worried, for the tempo of air operations was maintained throughout that day – and the next too, for Christmas Eve was fine and clear and the Tempests were once again called upon to lend their support in the Ardennes sector. Every Allied fighter-bomber seemed to be in the air during the hours of daylight, striking hard at concentrations of enemy troops, transport and armour wherever they were to be found. While more waves of C-47 transport aircraft dropped further supplies into Bastogne, their fighter-bomber escort worked methodically round the perimeter, bombing and rocketing German ground forces who were sometimes as close as fifty yards to the defences.

The air commitment was not all one-sided. Shortly before noon, dozens of bomb-carrying Focke-Wulfs and Messerschmitts suddenly appeared over the front, concentrating on Bastogne. While they hammered the perimeter, hundreds of Panzer Grenadiers in white snow suits, who had lain in hiding for many hours, crept forward into assault positions, and as soon as the air attack was over they charged the American defences in an all-out attempt to break through. They failed, and their commander, General Kokott, now knew for certain that he would never overrun the stubborn, gallant garrison, for it was now only a matter of hours before the arrival of American relief columns.

In the snow and the cold and the misery and the darkness, it was Christmas Day. But in the Ardennes, both sides were too busy fighting to care.

Wing Commander George Yeoman spent his Christmas Day crouching miserably in the ruins of what had once been a signal box beside the Venlo–Nijmegen railway line, four miles north of Boxmeer. Two miles away to the west, British soldiers were no doubt trying to forget the war for a few hours while they enjoyed whatever Christmas comforts they could lay their hands on. In half an hour of fast walking, he could be with them.

There was one snag. Between himself and the British lines was a long wood, flanked on one side by a road and on the other by a river, and it was full of Germans.

On the western fringe of the wood, facing the British lines, the Germans had set up a formidable array of strongly-fortified positions containing deadly 88-mm anti-tank guns, heavy howitzers and machine-guns, completely dominating the mile or so of open ground beyond. Tanks and infantry attempting to cross that open ground would be subjected to a staggering weight of fire. It would be suicide, even for an army.

But one man might just get across, if the conditions were right.

An unnamed guide had brought Yeoman from the former priest's house to his present location the night before. The Dutch had helped him all they could, providing him with warm clothing, a bundle of food and some brandy to stave off the bitter cold, and briefing him as fully as they could on the extent of the German positions in the wood. They could do no more, and he vowed that if he survived the ordeal of the next few hours, he would some day return in happier times and express his gratitude in tangible terms: not that those gallant, unselfish people would expect it of him.

From his hiding-place – a tiny burrow amid a pile of fallen masonry and beams – Yeoman had been able to get some idea of the ground that lay ahead of him. Through a hole in the tumbled bricks, he had seen a good deal of enemy movement on the road that flanked the wood over to his right, but no movement at all on the strip of ground immediately in front of him, between the railway line and the eastern fringe of the trees. From the railway line, the ground sloped gently away and then levelled out; several dark tracks wandered through the snow towards the river away to the left and he studied them carefully, knowing that they were small streams and that the ground around them, beneath the snow, was marshy and treacherous.

So, lying in his hole, he planned his route as carefully as he could, estimating the number of paces to the edge of the wood and to each of the streams he would have to negotiate. Once inside the wood, it would be a matter of luck and of stealth; he would force himself to move quietly and carefully, from tree to tree and on his belly if he had to.

The Germans, he felt sure, would be more relaxed than usual. There was no immediate threat in this sector, and it was Christmas. He tried to put himself in the place of the enemy troops guarding this lonely stretch of wood and marshland, to feel as they would feel, so near and yet so far away from home. They would be trying to forget the war for a few hours, and their emotions would be a mixture of nostalgia, homesickness and perhaps discontentment that it was their turn for front-line duty, when their comrades in the rear area could at least sleep dry and warm, instead of in makeshift dugouts covered with logs and earth and camouflaged tarpaulins. Whatever their feelings, they would be unlikely to suspect that a solitary British airman was moving cautiously in their midst.

For Yeoman, the daylight hours of that Christmas Eve seemed never-ending. Cramped and frozen, he thought longingly of the warm fire he had left behind in the ex-priest's house, and dreamed of the hot, plentiful food of bygone Christmases. He wondered what his father, John Yeoman, was doing at that moment, in his little cottage not far from the ancient market town of Richmond, in north Yorkshire. There would be a goose for Christmas dinner; there always had been, for as long as Yeoman could remember, with all the trimmings.

The light was beginning to fade at last. The sky was still clear, but there was no moon, for which the pilot was thankful. Nevertheless, the icy diamonds of the stars shed enough light for the dark figure of a man, moving across the snowy ground, to be picked out by a sharp-eyed sentry. . . . Well, that was a risk he would have to take. He would have to bank on the likelihood that all the sentries would be looking the other way.

He ate the last of the small supply of food the former priest had given him and finished the brandy, looking regretfully at the empty bottle for a moment or two before burying it among the stones. Then, crawling from his burrow, he cautiously stood upright and looked around, flexing his aching limbs.

Over to the right, where the road flanked the wood half a mile away, there was the sound of a motor-cycle engine. The noise swelled, carrying clearly on the frosty air and seeming dangerously close, then died away in the distance. Apart from that, the night was silent.

He began to walk down the slope, measuring his steps carefully, stopping every now and then to listen. To his surprise and relief, he found that the streams he had seen earlier were narrow, and that he could easily jump over them; he had not relished the prospect of having to wade through icy water.

One of the streams seemed to wend its way directly towards the wood and he decided to follow it, reasoning that it probably flowed right through to the other side. This stream too was narrow, but it had carved quite a deep little gully for itself out of the soft ground; it would afford excellent cover if Yeoman ran into any danger.

The ground was level now, and the trees loomed darkly ahead of him. He crouched down low and listened intently again, and now, for the first time, heard sounds that told him the wood was occupied; a faint clank of metal, the distant throb of a generator.

A short thirty-yard sprint brought him into the outer fringe of the wood and he stood there for a good five minutes in the shelter of a tree trunk, willing his breathing to become steadier and his heart to cease its hammering. Then he moved forward again, stealing from tree to tree, checking his little luminous escape compass from time to time to make sure that he was always heading west. It was just as well he had the compass, for he had been wrong about the stream; after a while, it curved away to the left and vanished.

Voices came suddenly out of the darkness and he froze, his face pressed against the rough bark of a fir tree while he tried to pin-point the exact direction from which the sound was coming. Then, ahead and a little way to the right, he saw a brief glow of yellow light and the dark shape of a man's figure silhouetted against it as someone lifted the covering that hung over the entrance of a dugout and stepped outside.

There was a grunt, a lengthy splashing of water as the man relieved himself against a tree, followed by a contented sigh. A moment later the light glowed again, to be immediately extinguished as the covering over the dugout entrance was replaced.

Yeoman went on, taking care to give the dugout a wide berth. He could hear the dull murmur of several voices now, and knew that he must be passing right through the middle of the garrison's living quarters. As he walked slowly on, fighting down the panic-stricken urge to cast caution to the winds and break into a run, he heard someone start to sing in a high, clear voice:

'Stille Nacht, heilige Nacht, Alles schläft, einsam wacht nur das traute, hochheilige Paar . . .' And, one by one, other voices joined in, softly at first, then swelling together until it seemed as though the carol filled the night:

'. . . Holder Knabe mit lockigem Haar, schlaf' in himmlischer Ruhe, schlaf' in himmlischer Ruh' . . .'

Sing! Yeoman prayed wildly to himself, think of all the carols in the world and sing them! He began to walk faster, almost recklessly, stumbling a little as he moved from tree to tree. The voices gradually receded behind him and he forced himself to slow down once more, stopping again to take in breath.

He smelt cigar smoke, saw the red glow in the night and the dark shape of a man all in the same instant.

'Johann,' a voice said softly out of the darkness. *'Ist das Johann? Du bist verspätet. Komm', unser Feldwebel is weggegangen und wir haben Schnaps and Zigarren. Mach' schnell, mensch, ehe er zurück-kommt!'*

Yeoman took a deep breath, then muttered in what he hoped was a recognizable German accent:

'Nein, es ist nicht Johann. Ich bin Hans Schneider.' He

plucked the name out of thin air. *'Frohliche Weihnachten,'* he added desperately, wishing the other a happy Christmas.

There was a momentary silence. Then, as Yeoman tried to sidle away into the shadows, the German soldier said suspiciously:

Schneider? Ich kenne kein Schneider hier. Wer sind Sie? Und wohin gehen Sie?'

Yeoman knew instinctively that he had no hope of bluffing his way out of the present situation. His German, although fairly adequate, would not stand up to a prolonged conversation without betraying some trace of an English accent.

He took a few paces towards the German soldier, giving a parody of a friendly chuckle. He saw the vague white blur of the man's face and lashed out with all his strength, striking him just under the nose with the heel of his hand. There was the sickening crunch of shattering bone and the soldier gave a strangled cry, staggering back to cannon off a tree trunk and then fall like a log.

Yeoman threw himself on top of him, rolling him over and hooking his right arm under the German's chin. Then, ramming his knee into the small of the soldier's back, he clasped his hands and exerted upward pressure. The German struggled frantically, his hands scrabbling at Yeoman as he tried to reach back over his shoulders to grip his attacker.

There was a crack like a breaking twig as the man's spine snapped. His clawing hands fluttered aimlessly and violent tremors ran through his body. Then, after a series of spasmodic jerks, he was still.

Yeoman stood up, breathing heavily, and dragged the body into the shadows. He would have liked to hide it properly, but there was no undergrowth in this coniferous wood and it was the best he could do.

Some distance away, the dead man's colleagues were still singing. Yeoman leaned against a tree for a moment, feeling sick; it was the first time he had killed a man with his bare hands, and it was not a pleasant sensation. Then, pulling himself together with an effort, he turned away and resumed his trek through the wood. He knew now that he had nothing to lose; if the enemy captured him now, he could expect no mercy.

He walked on for several more minutes, until the trees ahead of him began to thin out visibly. He paused when he heard more voices, melting into the shadows, and stood trembling for some time while he assessed the situation.

Peering into the darkness, he made out several low mounds between the trees. They puzzled him for a moment, until he realized that he was looking at gun emplacements with camouflage netting draped over them. The gun crews must be somewhere near at hand, presumably in the communal bunker – that must be the source of the voices, he thought – but he could not locate it. Neither could he see any sentries, although he guessed that they must be positioned forward of the guns in observation posts along the fringe of the wood.

He dropped on to his belly and began to worm his way forward, stopping frequently. Very little snow had filtered through the dense branches of the conifers; the ground was soft and moist, inches thick in mould, and Yeoman was able to crawl in silence, carefully reaching ahead before every move to brush aside tell-tale twigs that might have betrayed his presence.

He inched his way past one of the gun pits, so close that he could see the long barrel of the 88-mm poking out from its protective camouflage. Then, suddenly, there were no more trees ahead of him.

Panic gripped him as he looked out over the flat, featureless snowscape. There were no hiding places, no friendly shadows, no sheltering gullies – nothing at all until the eye alighted on the dark shadow of another line of trees, over a mile away. Beyond those trees, Yeoman knew, were the forward positions of the British Second Army; but how he was going to reach them he had no idea.

For a long time he lay there, curled up in the blackness between the roots of a great pine tree, overwhelmed by black despair. He could not go on, because some sentry would be sure to spot him against the blank background; neither could he stay where he was, for there was nowhere to hide in the wood and daylight would certainly bring discovery. His Dutch friends had been right. He had no chance of getting through.

He should have stayed with them, in comparative safety, until the Allies broke through . . .

A klaxon howled, sending a silent scream of fear through him. He curled up tighter into a ball as the strident noise went on endlessly and the wood erupted into life. All around him, out of the very ground it seemed, soldiers came spilling from hidden bunkers, shouting orders. Feet thudded past him, only yards away.

The klaxon ceased its din. Amid shouts and curses, the soldiers were stripping the camouflage netting from their guns. Yeoman raised a cautious head and looked at the nearest of the weapons; in the gloom, he was able to make out that the barrel was being elevated, its muzzle pointing at an angle towards the sky.

Rising above the clamour around him, he heard the unmistakable drone of aero-engines. Soon the night was throbbing with sound, and he knew that high above his head the Pathfinders of RAF Bomber Command were leading yet another massive attack towards the battered industries of the Ruhr.

The beams of searchlights, situated somewhere to the rear, began to probe the sky. A few moments later, the 88-mm guns along the edge of the wood opened up simultaneously with an ear-splitting crash. Yeoman cowered away involuntarily from the fearful noise as the guns hurled salvo after salvo of shells into the night, splitting the darkness with the red flashes from their muzzles.

Suddenly, like a revelation, he knew that this was his chance – perhaps his only chance. Jumping quickly to his feet he ran through the outer fringe of trees and into the open plain beyond. No one challenged him, though with every step he expected to hear the chatter of a machine-gun and feel the violent impact of bullets.

The icy air tore at his lungs as he ran, striving to put as much distance between himself and the German positions before he was spotted. The crash and roar of the guns continued behind him and shrapnel whined down all around, slapping into the snow to lie hissing as it cooled.

He zig-zagged frantically as he ran, trying to make himself as difficult a target as possible. The breath sobbed in his throat and the far wood seemed as distant as ever. Twice he stumbled and fell headlong, staggering to his feet again to continue his dash for freedom. He felt utterly alone and exposed, like a fly on white wallpaper.

The glare of the searchlights made the night as bright as day. High overhead, among the bomber stream, clusters of shell bursts flashed and sparkled.

Suddenly, a white light filled the sky. Yeoman hurled himself flat, clawing at the frozen snow in a vain effort to make himself less conspicuous. Above him, a white flare drifted slowly down. It landed on the snow fifty yards away and lay sputtering faintly.

A machine-gun hammered and tracer flashed through the night, the bullets probing in an arc over his head. He cringed in the snow, his eyes tightly shut, and waited for the end.

Then, suddenly, he opened his eyes again as an incredible fact dawned on him. The machine-gun fire was coming from somewhere ahead of him. Raising his head a few inches, he screamed:

'Don't shoot! For God's sake hold your fire! I'm English!'

The machine-gun hammered briefly again, then ceased abruptly as though on someone's orders. A shout came through the night from the line of trees in front of him.

'Who are you? Identify yourself!'

The pilot swallowed in an attempt to moisten his dry throat and cried hoarsely:

'Yeoman. Wing Commander, Royal Air Force.'

'All right,' the voice in the darkness answered him, 'come on forward. But keep low – you are still in range of the Jerry machine-guns. And keep your hands on your head until we've had a look at you.'

Yeoman did as he was told. There was utter silence once more as he moved forward; the bombers had droned away into the distance and the guns had stopped firing.

'Right, that's far enough. Stay where you are, and don't take your hands off your head.'

Two soldiers, both carrying sub-machine-guns, emerged from the shadow of the trees and faced the pilot.

'You'd better be who you say you are,' one of them said menacingly. His companion gave a grunt that might have passed for a chuckle.

'I reckon he's genuine enough,' he said. 'Who else but an Air Force bloke would be stupid enough to run through a Jerry minefield?'

Yeoman's legs suddenly gave way under him and he collapsed at the feet of the two men. They moved hastily aside as he vomited into the snow.

9

By nightfall on 26 December, it was clear that the German offensive in the Ardennes had failed. At 1700 on that Tuesday afternoon, the spearhead of the US 4th Armoured Division reached Bastogne and secured the highway, enabling the first supply convoys to move in.

But the Germans still had plenty of fight left in them, and they still had a few tricks up their sleeve. On the morning of the twenty-seventh, as it was not possible to bring all the necessary supplies in by the single road that was open, the Americans laid on one last air-drop.

Thirteen C-47 transports came winging in from the west, towing gliders, and flew straight into the concentrated fire of a line of anti-aircraft guns set up along their flight path by the Hermann Göring Flak Regiment. Nine of the C-47s went down in flames, though all of them managed to cast off their gliders in time and the latter landed within the perimeter.

The Germans now set about a defensive front by pulling back and re-grouping what was left of their armoured divisions. These had taken a fearful battering, losing 530 tanks – most of which, undamaged in the actual fighting, had had to be abandoned through lack of fuel because the airborne forces had failed to seize and hold on to vital American fuel dumps. Yet still the Germans strove to capture Bastogne. Division after division was sent up, arriving successively in the Bastogne area to be committed against the town. At one stage, the siege of Bastogne occupied no fewer than nine German divisions, completely frustrating any chances of a further counter-attack.

The Allied fighter-bombers were everywhere, probing deep

behind the enemy lines, destroying trains and convoys and armour wherever they were to be found. And the German soldiers, cowering in the snow and the mud of the ditches alongside the bomb- and bullet-swept roads, shook their fists and cursed their own airmen bitterly; for suddenly, mysteriously, the Luftwaffe seemed to have vanished from the sky. . . .

The general was a young man, although his hair had broad grey streaks in it and sharp lines were etched across his face. He smoked cigars incessantly, lighting a fresh one with the stub of another. Now, under the harsh glare of the lights in the underground operations room, he surveyed the wing commanders of the Luftwaffe's 2nd Air Division, who stood in a semicircle around a large table. Covering it, under a glass top, was a map of western and northern Germany, part of France and the Low Countries.

The general chewed thoughtfully on his cigar and then removed it, placing it carefully in an ashtray. His eyes roved round the circle of pilots, all young men also, all much decorated. He studied each face intently for a few seconds, then gave a tired smile.

'Gentlemen,' he said, 'we have known each other for a long time. You will not misunderstand me, I am sure, when I say that things are not going well for us.'

There were murmurs of assent around the table. The general went on to voice their own thoughts.

'The offensive in the Ardennes has failed. We have lost more tanks and troops than we can affored and now we are once more on the defensive. This being the case, you are doubtless wondering why offensive Luftwaffe operations along most of the Western Front have been suspended since yesterday, at the very time when our forces are most in need of them.'

The wing commanders exchanged glances. The general picked up his cigar, puffed at it several times to get it going, then laid it aside once more. A cloud of pungent grey smoke drifted over the map.

'The reason, gentlemen,' he went on, 'is quite simple. Within the next twenty-four hours, the Luftwaffe squadrons in the west will be privileged to strike the biggest blow against the Allied air forces since the offensive of 1940.'

Triumphantly, the general noted the effect of his words on the men who confronted him. Their faces registered expressions that ranged from enthusiasm to frank disbelief.

'Over the past few days,' the general told them, 'fresh fighter and fighter-bomber squadrons have been quietly moved to the north-west from other sectors. You are all aware of these moves, for the new units have temporarily been placed under your command. What you have not been told, until this moment, is the overall strategy behind the re-organization.

'At first light tomorrow morning, New Year's Day, more than one thousand Focke-Wulfs and Messerschmitts will attack sixteen Allied airfields in Holland and Belgium. The attack will be code-named Operation Hermann.'

He paused for dramatic effect. A buzz like an electric current ran through his audience. Someone gave a low whistle, and the general smiled again. Then, suddenly businesslike, he leaned over the map, his jabbing index finger pointing out the German airfields on which the strike aircraft were now massed.

'Apeldoorn – Ahlhorn – Twenthe – Münster – Lippstadt – Rheine – Neuenkirchen – Metelen – Harskamp – Teuge – Varrelbusch – and all their satellite fields. Eleven of our finest fighter wings, gentlemen. Jagdgeschwader 2, JG-3, JG-4, JG-5, JG-26, JG-27, JG-52, JG-53, JG-54, JG-66 and JG-301. All with proud records stretching back to our earliest victories. Ah, those were the days, gentlemen, and now we have a chance to recapture them!'

He went on to outline the plan, which was masterly in its conception. For some time, Luftwaffe Intelligence had known that the C-in-C of the RAF's 2nd Tactical Air Force, Air Marshal Sir Arthur Coningham, had been forced because of weather and logistics difficulties to concentrate his forces on a comparatively small number of airfields.

'At Eindhoven, for example, there are known to be no fewer than six squadrons – two of Tempests, one of Spitfires and three of Typhoons. The point is that the British do not consider such a concentration to be unduly hazardous; over the past couple of months, regrettably, the appearance of our aircraft over their airfields has been almost as rare as snow in summer, and they have grown complacent. Well, we are about to shake their complacency to its roots!'

The general lit a fresh cigar, then said:

'We know for a fact that a lot of their heavy anti-aircraft defences have been withdrawn, and that they no longer use camouflage netting to conceal their aircraft. Your pilots should therefore have no difficulty in locating their targets.

'Now to the finer details. Some of you may be feeling that you would have liked more time to plan the operation, but such was the need for strict security that it was decided not to pass on any information, even to your level of command, until a few hours before the operation was due to take place.'

The general noticed that one or two of his wing commanders were looking slightly worried, and hastily reassured them.

'All the planning has been done for you. You will all be given target folders shortly, but you are not under any circumstances to open them until 0300 hours tomorrow morning, when you may brief your squadron commanders. All I can tell you at this stage is that the attack formation will be divided into three waves, each of which will be led by a Junkers 188 night fighter which will be responsible for accurate navigation and for maintaining communications with Air Division HQ.

'The first wave will fly a long curve out over the north coast of Holland, staying low over the sea and then turning in over the Zuider Zee to attack airfields in the Brussels area. The second wave will come in at ground level in the Arnhem sector and strike at RAF airfields in Holland, while the third wave, also at ground level, will approach through Venlo and attack airfields in the US Ninth Army sector. By coming in at low level, we hope to escape detection by enemy radar and so achieve complete surprise.'

The general, who had been leaning forward with his palms on the table top, now straightened up abruptly and stood with his hands behind his back.

'I shall not ask you if you have any questions, gentlemen,' he concluded, 'because in any case I am not at liberty to answer them. It only remains for me to wish you good luck.'

He shook hands solemnly with every one of them. After they had saluted and left the room, he went to his office and locked the door, for he did not wish to be disturbed.

Gradually, the room filled with cigar smoke. The general stared fixedly into it, lost in his thoughts. Foremost in his mind was the sure knowledge that he would never again see some of the young men who had just left him; men who had served under his command at one time or another from the Channel to Stalingrad. By this time tomorrow, they would be dead.

By this time tomorrow, too, the Luftwaffe would have played its last trump card. Beyond that, there would be nothing but fire and ruin and the final plunge, like a meteor, to destruction.

He opened his desk drawer and took out a Luger automatic. It shone dully in the light. For a few moments he weighed it in his hand, savouring the feel of it; it had been with him for a long time now and was an inseparable part of him, by his side constantly, like a loving mistress.

He caressed its cold metal with his fingertips, then gave a deep sigh and laid it carefully back in the desk drawer. It would survive Germany's defeat; he would not. Vaguely, he wondered who would own the Luger one day. An English officer, maybe. He hoped that whoever it was would take care of it, and not leave it to rust in some attic, a forgotten souvenir.

He shrugged and rose abruptly, putting the thoughts from his mind. There was still work to be done, and very little time in which to do it.

After celebrating his return Yeoman sat in 505 Squadron's dispersal hut, warming his outstretched hands against a red-hot stove. Tim Phelan and a few other pilots were also present, reading, playing cards or just dozing in armchairs. It was 1600 hours in the afternoon of the last day of 1944; outside it was snowing, and in less than half an hour it would be pitch black.

'I don't know why you bother to hang around,' Phelan said suddenly. 'You've been grounded since you got back, and you're going on leave tomorrow; if I were you, I'd be in my nice, comfortable bed, catching up on some sleep.'

The mere mention of sleep made Yeoman yawn involuntarily. He put a hand over his mouth and smiled.

'I suppose it's as comfortable here as anywhere else, Tim,' he said. 'At least it's warm.' He paused and, as he always did when in an uncertain mood, took out his pipe and began to fill it methodically.

'To tell you the truth,' he went on, 'I'm uneasy. I can't shake off this strange feeling that something's about to happen. Something quite disastrous. Call it a sixth sense if you like, but . . .'

Phelan laughed, interrupting him. 'Only we Irish are allowed to have a sixth sense,' he said, 'and I haven't heard any banshees wailing lately. No, George, I have a feeling that you're suffering from reaction. You're very lucky to be with us, you know.'

Yeoman nodded. 'I know. I don't think it's anything to do with that, though.' Abruptly, he changed the subject. 'Where were you last New Year's Eve, Tim?'

'On leave, in Ireland. I cut it short, though. Felt a bit guilty, being out of uniform and tucking into masses of ham and eggs and drinking stout until it was running out of my ears.'

He paused for a moment, looking a little embarrassed. Then he said:

'No, that wasn't the real reason. A lot of people over there hate the British, George. I was asked more than once why I was fighting somebody else's war. I tried to explain that it was because I love flying more than anything else, not to mention a bit of excitement, but they didn't seem to understand.'

Phelan's brow furrowed in perplexity for a moment, then he went on:

'Oddly enough, the only people who did understand were the fellers who'd fought against the British in the 1920s, back in the time of the Troubles. They don't hate the British, George, at least most of them don't. But there are an awful lot of pro-German bastards in Ireland just at the moment, make no mistake about it. Anyway, I had a pretty lousy Christmas and New Year, to cut a long story short. What about you?'

'I was commanding 380 Squadron then,' Yeoman answered, 'flying Mosquitos. We'd just clobbered a Jerry airfield where they were testing rocket fighters – you know, these Messerschmitt 163s we've been hearing about lately – so the whole squadron, or what was left of it, was stood down for a couple of weeks.'

He opened the door of the stove with a long piece of metal, picked up a log of wood and dropped it inside. Sparks scattered up the flue.

'I don't think any of us went home,' he said, 'except for one or two who had wives and families. Instead, we went to London and got thoroughly pissed. Never saw daylight for a fortnight; we'd go to some booze-up or other, get back to our hotel in the small hours, sleep all day and get up again after dark. I don't really remember much about it at all. I suppose it did us all the world of good,' he added dubiously.

There was a blast of cold air, a flurry of snow, and Simon Wynne-Williams burst into the hut, quickly closing the door behind him. Reverently, he deposited two bottles of whisky on the trestle table in the middle of the room.

'I didn't think there was much chance of any flying,' he said, 'so I thought we'd splice the mainbrace, as the Navy says.' He looked at Yeoman and raised a questioning eyebrow. 'Senior officer's permission to open the bar?'

'Too true,' Yeoman said enthusiastically. Tin mugs appeared as if by magic and the pilots clustered round the table as Wynne-Williams doled out the golden liquid.

'I've given a couple of bottles to the ground crews as well,' he said. 'Poor sods are just about frozen stiff. Anyway, as duty pilot I took it upon myself to order them to picket the aircraft for the night and get into the warm.'

Yeoman nodded. 'That was good thinking.' He looked appreciatively at the liquid in his mug and swallowed some, feeling its warm glow beginning to spread through him. 'To think,' he said, 'that I used to hate this stuff.'

Phelan drank also. 'Well,' he said, 'here's to the next New Year's Eve spent anywhere else than in Holland!'

'Oh, Lord,' someone moaned in mock dismay, 'don't say that – we'll probably end up in Japan!'

'You know what I mean,' the Irishman chuckled. He turned to Yeoman and said:

'Do you think it might be an idea to invite a few Dutch civilians back to the mess tonight for some drinks? You know, the people who've been especially good to us.'

Yeoman shook his head firmly. 'No, I don't think that would be a good idea at all. We can't invite all of them, and those we miss out would be bound to be jealous – it could well create friction among the population of Eindhoven, and we don't want that. What we'll do, instead, is dish out some goodies tomorrow for the kids – as much chocolate as we can spare, and so on. I think that would be more to the point.'

The others nodded in agreement. The pinched, hungry look of the Dutch children was something none of them had got used to.

The door opened again, admitting another freezing blast, and a flight sergeant came into the room, muffled up in a great-coat, scarf and balaclava helmet. He came over to the stove and addressed Yeoman. Snow fell off him and melted in little pools at his feet.

'Got 'em all bedded down for the night, sir,' he said, referring to the aircraft. 'Only two unserviceable, 519 and 636.'

Yeoman nodded. 'Thanks, Chief. Are your lads okay?'

'A bit cold, sir, but they're all indoors now and they'll soon thaw out. They're looking forward to celebrating the New Year, sir. Let's hope it's better than the last one.'

'I'll drink to that,' Yeoman grinned. 'Have a drop of whisky, Chief?'

'Thanks, sir. Don't mind if I do.'

The flight sergeant took the proffered bottle and poured a liberal measure into a mug someone handed to him. He stood close to the stove, warming himself, and said to the wing commander:

'You know that there's an invitation for the officers to come over to the sergeants' mess tonight, sir?'

Yeoman nodded. 'We'll be there, Chief,' he promised. 'About nine o'clock, if that's all right. We'll stay for an hour or so.'

'Fine, sir.' The flight sergeant finished his whisky and set down the mug. 'I'll be on my way, then. We'll see you later, gentlemen.'

He turned towards the door, and as he did so the telephone shrilled. The watchkeeper, a corporal, who had been sitting unobtrusively in a corner reading a book, lifted the receiver.

'Hold on a minute, Chief,' Yeoman said to the flight sergeant. 'I've a feeling this might be something that concerns you, too.'

'It's GCC for you, sir,' the corporal said, holding out the instrument. Yeoman took it and listened for a couple of minutes, then said in an angry tone: 'Why us, for Christ's sake?'

There was utter silence in the dispersal hut, except for the crackle of the wood in the stove. Everyone could hear the metallic whisper of the voice on the other end of the line.

Quietly, Yeoman said, 'I see', and replaced the receiver. The others looked at him expectantly. They knew from his expression what was coming.

'I'm afraid our New Year party has had it, chaps,' he said. 'GCC wants us to carry out a maximum-strength sweep in the Cologne area at dawn tomorrow; primarily, we'll be shooting up trains. So two pints, no more, and to bed by ten o'clock. I'm afraid we're going to have to give the sergeants' mess a miss, Chief. Briefing at 0600. Life's a bastard, isn't it?'

10

The Luftwaffe wing commander was burning with fury. For days now, his unit had been hopping from one airfield to another; the last move had come two days after Christmas, and his pilots had barely started to settle down in their new home when, at 1600 hours on New Year's Eve – just as they had all been looking forward to a pleasantly drunken evening – the order had come for them to move off again.

Any fool, just by looking out of the window, could tell that flying was out of the question. Visibility was appalling, with low cloud and snow showers, and there was a strong, gusty wind. The wing commander telephoned headquarters, located a staff officer and proceeded to tell him exactly what he thought of chairbound idiots who had no idea what it was like to fly single-seat fighters in conditions such as these.

The staff officer was adamant. He sympathized with the wing commander, but no, he could do nothing to change the orders, which came from the very highest authority. And no, he could not tell the wing commander where they were going; his pilots would receive instructions over the radio as soon as they were airborne.

Sixty Focke-Wulf 190s took off from their base near Emden into the grey twilight, circling for a long time in driving snow until they were in reasonable formation. The wing commander had received orders to switch to the divisional fighter control frequency, and now, over the radio, a curt voice told him to set course 180 degrees. There was nothing else.

The formation turned southwards, the three squadrons flying in line astern in the narrow corridor between the lowering cloud base and the mist-shrouded hilltops of the Teutoburger

Forest. It grew steadily darker and the snow whirled down in great flakes, clinging to the perspex of the windscreens so that, despite the constant swishing of the wipers, it was almost impossible to see ahead.

To make matters worse, the low altitude at which the fighters were flying meant that all radio contact with the outside world had been lost. The formation groped its way blindly on through the cloud, mist and snow, the pilot of each aircraft clinging desperately to the navigation lights of the one ahead and the two or three he was able to see in the murk on either side of him.

The inevitable happened with terrifying speed. There was a sudden vivid flash, a rolling ball of flame in the semi-darkness as one of the fighters in the lowest group hit the ground and exploded.

The wing commander pounded his fist against the instrument panel in impotent rage, venting his fury against those who had ordered this nightmare journey in a string of obscene oaths.

To hell with it! He was going to bring his men down to land, no matter where. Over his radio, he instructed his squadron leaders to keep their eyes open for an airfield.

A few minutes later, more by good luck than anything else, they sighted Rheine-Hopsten airfield. The wing commander ordered his squadrons to land one after the other, the pilots circling the airfield slowly as they awaited their turn.

Fifty out of the original sixty fighters got down, although some of these were damaged when they ground-looped on the icy runways. Of the ten machines that were missing, the wing commander knew that one had definitely crashed; the remainder, it was later learned, had lost contact with the formation and had flown on, hopelessly lost, until they ran out of fuel. Too low to bale out, the pilots had tried to crash-land as best they could. Five of them were dead or seriously injured.

Such was the story the wing commander from Emden, ashen-faced and trembling as he drank glass after glass of schnaps in the officers' mess, told Oberstleutnant Joachim Richter, commander of Jagdgeschwader 66. Gently, Richter restrained him from taking any more of the fiery spirit.

'You mean you really have no idea why you were ordered down here?' he asked in surprise. The other shook his head.

'None whatsoever. They just ordered us to take off virtually at a moment's notice, the murdering bastards, and fly south. I want to use the telephone! Somebody's head is going to roll because of what my boys have just been through!'

Richter laid his hand on the irate man's arm. 'I'm afraid that's out of the question, old chap. There are to be no outgoing or incoming calls of any kind until further notice. Those are our orders. And no drinking after 1800 hours, either,' he added, looking meaningfully at the wing commander's glass.

The wing commander placed it carefully on the bar, then said:

'Look, just what the devil is going on? I'd appreciate it if somebody would put me in the picture.'

Richter knew that for security reasons, only the commanders of the airfields where the attack aircraft were to be temporarily based, such as himself, had received any kind of briefing at all. No one else was to be given any kind of information until the main briefing, which was to take place at 0300 in the morning. This was as much as he was permitted to tell the new arrivals, who, considerably disgruntled, went off to snatch a few hours' sleep.

Three hours into New Year's Day 1945 the briefing-room at Rheine – which, in common with much else, had been moved underground for comparative safety from Allied bombing – was packed to capacity. The assembled pilots literally sat on the edges of their seats, all their grievances forgotten, as Richter gave them the details of the great air attack in which they would soon take part.

The 250 fighters based on Rheine-Hopsten and its satellite airfields were to attack several RAF airfields in Holland, the most important of which was Eindhoven. The whole mission was to be flown at less than six hundred feet, and strict radio silence was to be maintained until the target area was reached. The fast Junkers 188 pathfinder aircraft would lead the massive formation to within a few miles of the target area, by which time it would be light enough for the fighter pilots to carry out their own visual navigation.

The pilots were issued with maps which had the courses and various pin-points already marked on them. They were also given a set of printed instructions on a card, which reduced their forthcoming task to its bare essentials:

> 1. Everything counts. 2. At start point, switch on radio. Switch on weapons. Switch on navigation lights. 3. Maintain discipline when attacking. 4. Pay particular attention to damaged and burning aircraft. Count them in your score. 5. Do not forget to test your weapons before every strafing run. 6. Keep a sharp lookout for airfields during your approach and return flights and make a note of their location.

The briefing over, the pilots made for their messes to try and force down some food, although few of them had any appetite. There was hardly any talking, and the mess waiters in their white jackets moved on tiptoe between the tables. When one of them accidentally dropped a fork with a clatter, a hundred pairs of eyes turned towards him accusingly. The man blushed bright red and scurried away – and then, suddenly, the tension was broken.

'You'd think the poor sod had farted in church,' grinned Johnny Schumacher, who sat in his accustomed place opposite Richter. The latter smiled and pushed his plate aside, half the food on it untouched.

'I'll be glad when this show's over,' he said, looking at his watch, 'and we can all go back to bed again. I'm so tired I can hardly stand up. If you've finished eating, we'll go and take a look at the weather.'

All over north-west Germany, the same scenes were being enacted. From airfield after airfield, in the pre-dawn darkness, the squadrons of Focke-Wulfs and Messerschmitts were taking off with a roar of engines that rattled the roof-tops of nearby towns and villages and brought their inhabitants startled from their sleep. One by one the great formations joined up over their airfields, and when all were in position the leaders took station behind the twinkling navigation lights of the pathfinder aircraft.

The first formation to set course, because it had the farthest to fly, was that scheduled to attack the complex of airfields around Brussels. The three hundred aircraft in this wave sped low over the sea; then, as dawn was beginning to streak the sky, it curved southwards over the Dutch coast.

It was here that flak claimed its first victims. Not Allied flak, but German. Either because it had been overlooked in the planning, or because of security reasons, the High Command had failed to alert the coastal anti-aircraft defences. Frantically, the fighter pilots fired off the recognition flares of the day, and the barrage tailed off – but not before three fighters had fallen burning from the winter sky. . . .

At Eindhoven, twenty Tempests taxied cautiously out towards the end of the runway, their pilots using their brakes gingerly on the icy surface. Yeoman, hands thrust deep into the pockets of his greatcoat, chin tucked in against the biting wind, watched them as they made their ungainly way and wished heartily that he was going with them. But the group commander had been quite adamant; Yeoman was under direct orders not to fly, and was to proceed on leave as soon as he could obtain a seat on one of the England-bound communications aircraft.

The first Tempests turned on to the runway and the throbbing, vibrating roar of their Sabre engines cut across the airfield as the pilots opened the throttles. Their dark shapes began to move, flitting past the lights of the flarepath.

Two by two, the powerful fighters lifted off the tarmac and climbed away to circle the field, joining up into their sections. The sky overhead was a beehive of navigation lights. Suddenly, the whole swarm wheeled away and set an eastward course towards where, on the horizon, a long grey line told of the approaching dawn. Yeoman watched them for a long time, until the thunder of their engines dwindled to a muted murmur, then went back into the operations trailer to join Wynne-Williams, who today was one of the two pilots detailed to remain at Eindhoven on readiness.

'Shall I get someone to run you back into town?' Wynne-Williams asked.

Yeoman shook his head, 'No, thanks. I'll wait until the lads get back. I'm not leaving until three o'clock this afternoon; there's plenty of time to pack my kit.'

The air over Eindhoven vibrated with sound again as more engines were run up on the far side of the airfield; one of the Canadian Typhoon squadrons was scheduled to take off shortly to lend support to the Allied ground forces who were still fighting hard in the Ardennes.

'It looks like being a hectic start to 1945,' Yeoman commented. He was to be proved right within the next few minutes, but not in the way he imagined.

The navigator of the Junkers 188 pathfinder aircraft, Richter thought, certainly knew his stuff. As the dawn light spread gradually behind the formation, and he began to pick out familiar landmarks, he saw that they had not strayed off course by as much as a kilometre.

The armada of Focke-Wulfs and Messerschmitts was over the River Maas now, just south of Nijmegen. Suddenly, the Ju 188 swung sharply to the right, rocking its wings and switching off its navigation lights, a clear indication to the following aircraft that they were on their own. It didn't matter; with only twenty miles to run to Eindhoven, and the light getting better all the time, they were likely to experience few problems in locating their target – or rather targets, for only sixty aircraft, led by Richter, were to hit Eindhoven. The remainder were to fly on to strike at Gilze-Rijen and other RAF airfields in Holland, so meticulously pin-pointed and photographed over the previous weeks by Me 262 reconnaissance jets.

As the kilometres flickered past under his wings, Richter, out at the head of the formation, meticulously checked that everything was in order. The engine sang sweetly, his cannon and machine-guns were armed and ready to fire. Down below, everything was calm and peaceful, as it always seemed to be on a New Year's morning, with the tiny houses and the windmills rising from the snow-covered landscape like features on a Christmas card.

For the first time in months, Richter felt completely at ease, even though the adrenalin was already pumping through his veins and all his senses were heightened by the prospect of action. He felt like singing. What a surprise the Tommies were going to get in just a few more minutes!

Suddenly, Eindhoven airfield was dead ahead.

Through the clear patch he had rubbed on the window of the operations trailer, Yeoman watched the Typhoons moving out of their dispersals on to the perimeter track, their wings laden with rocket projectiles. He wondered how many of them would come back; light flak, of which the enemy ground forces had plenty, took an appalling toll of the fighter-bomber squadrons.

Suddenly, the high-pitched scream of aero-engines under full power sliced through the frosty morning. Startled, Yeoman launched himself towards the door of the trailer and jumped down into the snow, transfixed for a moment by the sight that greeted him.

The streamlined shape of a 'long-nose' FW 190 flashed across the airfield, its nose and wings lit up by the flashes of its guns, so low that the blurring arc of its propeller seemed only inches from the ground. It was not alone; the sky was filled with German fighters, swarming over Eindhoven's eastern boundary.

The pilot of the leading Typhoon, which had just turned on to the runway, rammed open his throttle in a desperate attempt to get airborne. His wheels had just cleared the ground when cannon shells smashed into his aircraft, slamming it back down on the runway in a pile of blazing, tangled wreckage. A second Typhoon, also racing down the runway, ploughed into the wreck of the first and blew up. A few moments later, there was a terrific explosion as the rocket warheads of both fighters went off in the flames.

The pilots of the remaining Typhoons, bunched hopelessly together at the end of the runway or on the perimeter track, with no hope now of taking off, scrambled frantically from their cockpits. Some, gunning their engines and swinging their aircraft so that their noses pointed in the direction from which the attack was coming, opened up with their cannon, spraying the eastern sky in the vain hope of hitting something.

Wynne-Williams came tumbling from the operations trailer

a split second after Yeoman, just in time to see a speeding Focke-Wulf release two bombs into the airfield's fuel dump. There was a dull crump, a great balloon of flame, and then a column of twisting black smoke climbed slowly upwards.

'Come on!' Yeoman screamed, and hurled himself towards the nearer of the two Tempests which stood a few yards away in the readiness dispersal. As he ran, shedding his greatcoat, he saw out of the corner of his eye a series of vivid explosions over to the right, where 449 Squadron's Spitfires were dispersed. Then he was clawing his way desperately into the Tempest's cockpit, with only one thought in his mind; to get off the ground and fight.

Simon Wynne-Williams clambered into the second Tempest, narrowly beating the other readiness pilot, whose aircraft Yeoman had commandeered. Without bothering to fasten their seat harnesses, Yeoman and Wynne-Williams frantically cranked up their engines; both started after two or three tries with the usual bang and puff of oily smoke.

Looking across the airfield towards the columns of flame-shot smoke that rose from the burning Typhoons, Yeoman quickly assessed the situation. Running at an angle across the main runway, which was now completely blocked, was a much smaller subsidiary runway which was normally used only by communications aircraft. The Tempests would have to use it now, if they were to have any hope of getting off the ground.

The two Tempests taxied forward, Yeoman signalling his intentions by hand to Wynne-Williams. The wing commander wore no flying helment, so radio communication was impossible. The aircraft moved as rapidly as possible, zig-zagging furiously to present as difficult a target as possible, and Yeoman found himself cursing as he strove to prevent his heavy fighter from skidding off the perimeter track.

The two aircraft should have been easy meat as they waddled across the airfield, but to some extent they were screened from the marauding Focke-Wulfs by the drifting smoke and both reached the short runway without suffering any damage. All around them, parked aircraft and airfield installations continued to erupt in smoke and flame as the Focke-Wulfs made one strafing run after another, as yet unmolested by anti-aircraft fire of any kind.

It was now or never. Yeoman, followed closely by Wynne-Williams, pushed the throttle wide open and raised the tail as the speed built up. The main wheels bounced several times and he literally tore the Tempest off the ground, yanking up the undercarriage. He knew that his only chance was to try and get above the mêlée, so he held the fighter low down until he was doing close on 400 mph and then pulled back the stick, rocketing up in a near-vertical climb.

Still closely followed by Wynne-Williams, he came out of the climb at three thousand feet, just below the cloud base, and turned back towards Eindhoven, seeking targets against the snow-covered backdrop. They were not hard to find; the black outlines of the Focke-Wulfs stood out starkly as they zoomed and dived through the spreading pall of smoke, adding to the carnage all the time.

From Yeoman's vantage point the devastation wrought by the German fighters on Eindhoven seemed appalling – as indeed it was. The attack had lasted barely five minutes, and already almost every RAF fighter and fighter-bomber on the airfield was in flames, blazing furiously amid the crash of exploding bombs and the bark of the raiders' cannon. The lifeless bodies of airmen, mown down by shells and bullets, sprawled like broken dolls in the bloody snow.

Yeoman caught sight of two long-nosed Focke-Wulfs slipping low over the airfield boundary and went after them in a long dive, with Wynne-Williams on his left. The German fighters, made confident by the total absence of flak, were flying quite slowly, waggling their wings as they searched for likely targets, and the Tempests overhauled them easily.

There was no mistake. Yeoman fired, and the Focke-Wulf in his sights reared up sharply in front of his nose. Some fragments and several puffs of black smoke burst from it, then it turned over on its back, described a short parabola over the field and crashed near the blazing Typhoons.

The second Focke-Wulf, hit by Wynne-Williams, struck the ground the right way up in a great flurry of snow and slid over the frozen earth for a couple of hundred yards, shedding fragments of wing in all directions, before coming to rest with its nose buried in the side of one of 449 Squadron's dispersal huts. The pilot, white-faced and shaken to the bone, scrambled painfully from the cockpit and was promptly laid out by a right hook to the jaw delivered by an irate Canadian Spitfire pilot, who made the German his prisoner.

The two Tempests, meanwhile, flew slap through the middle of a group of Focke-Wulfs which were heading in the opposite direction and then climbed hard again, their pilots intending to repeat the previous manoeuvre. In this they were forestalled by Joachim Richter, who, having used up most of his ammunition, had been circling the airfield and guiding his pilots towards the few targets that were as yet untouched. He spotted the two Tempests, climbing like arrows towards the clouds, and detached half a dozen Focke-Wulfs to deal with them.

Yeoman and Wynne-Williams both saw them coming, and knew that they were going to have to fight for their lives. They also knew that they were going to have to rely entirely on their own wits to survive, since they had no radio contact with one another.

Resolutely, they turned to face the enemy.

Seventy miles south-east of Eindhoven, leading his formation of Tempests, Tim Phelan was puzzled. A few minutes earlier, listening to Group Central Control's frequency, he had picked up a frantic call from what, by the call sign it was using, sounded like an Auster army-cooperation aircraft. The message was fragmentary and disjointed, but to Phelan it seemed charged with menace.

'Large formation enemy . . . fifteen miles . . . Nijmegen . . . heading two-four-zero . . . unable to –'

The message ended there. Three times, Phelan tried to contact GCC, but because of the low altitude at which the Tempests were flying did not succeed in doing so.

For several minutes the Tempest formation continued to quarter the ground to the south-west of Cologne, searching for elusive trains, and then Phelan, his unease persisting, reached a decision. Pressing the R/T button, he told the others that he intended to take them to the north-west and patrol a line midway between Eindhoven and Rheine. The decision to ignore his operational orders and adopt another course of action was his alone; he prayed fervently that it was the right one.

He was falling, slowly and timelessly, like a wind-borne autumn leaf from the uppermost branches of a tall tree. There was no pain, no fear, no regret; just a profound sense that this moment was the fulfilment of everything.

Suddenly, in these last seconds, he saw everything with absolute clarity. There were no images of his past life, as they said there were supposed to be; but there were voices, some forgotten until this moment, of people he had once held dear. And there was a question, the answer to which no longer really mattered: how had this happened to him? There had been no smashing of bullets, no explosion or flash of flame. Just some flying débris, a great pause in time as though earth and sky had stood still for an instant, and then the plunge.

He supposed that he must have collided with something, but it didn't matter now. There was no way out, for he had no parachute. There had been no time, in the frantic rush to take off.

A dark patch on the snow, like a splash of spilled ink, rose in front of his eyes. It filled his entire vision beyond the windscreen. For a fleeting moment he wished that his last sight of the earth had been of something prettier and more colourful; of the spreading branches of a tree, perhaps, or a bed of flowers.

Then, suddenly, there were no more wishes; just a last great question that burst like a blinding light across the dwindling vestiges of his consciousness and refused to leave him, as though driving something of his lost self onward and upward in search of the ultimate answer. . . .

Over the pall of smoke that shrouded Eindhoven a lone Tempest circled, its wings and fuselage scarred and torn by bullets and shell splinters. Through eyes half-blinded by unashamed tears, the pilot peered down in search of a place to land.

The Focke-Wulfs had gone, their work of destruction complete, speeding away into the mist that covered the eastern horizon. By now the Allied anti-aircraft gunners were wide awake, and a storm of flak traced their path as they sped back towards the Rhine, knocking several of them from the sky. The remainder, sighing with relief as they entered their own territory, allowed themselves to relax a little, and to anticipate the luxury of a few hours' sleep between warm blankets.

It was a dangerous mistake. Phelan's Tempests, their cannon still unfired, caught the fleeing enemy north of Bocholt, and in a brief one-sided running battle – for few of the German pilots had any ammunition left – destroyed ten of them for no loss before being compelled to turn for home, short of fuel.

It was only now, as they entered Dutch territory, that the Tempest pilots began to have an idea of what had happened. They stared in horror at the huge columns of smoke that rose over their airfield and flew overhead, rocking their wings uncertainly as they wondered whether they would be able to land or not. In the end, Phelan made a low reconnaissance of a stretch of runway that seemed reasonably intact, and led his pilots down.

As they taxied in, they passed a huge smoking crater beside the edge of the runway. They had no idea, yet, that it contained the charred and mangled remains of a Tempest.

Carefully avoiding mounds of shattered aluminium that had once been aircraft, they taxied past the lakes of burning fuel, coughing as the acrid smoke penetrated their cockpits. One by one, they shut down their engines and climbed down into the churned-up slush, looking wordlessly at the devastation all around them.

Across the airfield Yeoman wandered aimlessly, bareheaded, his tunic flapping open despite the cold, ignoring the smoke that swirled around him. On his cheeks, dried tears formed pale tracks through the grime. He passed the torn wreckage of a Focke-Wulf and wandered on until he stood beside the crater that smouldered by the edge of the runway. A stench of burnt rubber and molten metal floated from its depths.

He stood there for a long time, brooding; then, like a dog shaking itself, he straightened his shoulders and began the long trek back towards the dispersal huts.

Later, a bulldozer would come along and shovel Dutch earth into the hole that mercifully concealed the mortal remains of Simon Wynne-Williams.

11

As the smoke clouds gradually thinned out and dispersed over the shattered airfields, the Allies began to count the cost of the German attack. It was bad enough. When the total was added up, it was found that 223 RAF and USAAF fighters and bombers had been reduced to scrap metal; thirty-five more non-operational types such as transport and communications aircraft had also been knocked out.

Eindhoven, attacked by Richter's excellently led Jagdgeschwader 66, had been one of the worst-hit targets. As well as the sixteen Typhoons which had been waiting to take off, the low-flying Focke-Wulfs had destroyed twenty-four other aircraft, including the twelve Spitfires of 449 Squadron. Is was sheer good fortune that the Tempests had escaped.

The airfields near Brussels were also badly hit. At Evere, in addition to four squadrons of Spitfires, there were dozens of other types ranging from Austers to Dakotas, all of them without camouflage netting, while at another field further up the road some sixty bombers were parked in straight lines, wing-tip to wing-tip.

Normally, a Spitfire patrol was flown from Evere at first light, but on this occasion there was some delay while the icy surface of the runway was sprinkled with grit. At 0900 the runway was judged safe for operations and two Spitfires took off to make a weather check, while twelve more taxied round the perimeter track. The first of these had just turned on to the runway when the first enemy fighters howled across the airfield.

What followed was utter chaos. Only one Spitfire managed to get airborne, and its gallant pilot, fighting against hopeless odds, destroyed a Messerschmitt before he in turn was shot down and killed. The remaining pilots scrambled for cover and watched helplessly as their aircraft were pulverized. Here, as at Eindhoven, there were no heavy anti-aircraft guns, and the few light ack-ack weapons that did open up soon ceased firing; they simply ran out of ammunition.

Everywhere, in the British and American sectors alike, it was the same story. Nevertheless, there was no doubt that the damage would have been much more extensive if all the German pilots had been of the same calibre as those belonging to Richter's Jagdgeschwader 66. As it was, many of the attackers flew erratically, became tangled up with their colleagues and showed extremely poor marksmanship, all of which tended to blunt the full fury of the attack. There were several instances of head-on collisions, and one of the airfield targets, in the American sector, was missed altogether.

Devastating though the blow had been to the Allied air forces, the Germans had suffered heavily too. The attack formations tended to straggle badly as they flew home, and one wave strayed over the formidable anti-aircraft defences covering the Scheldt Estuary, losing several of their number.

Allied fighters accounted for ninety-seven of the enemy. In addition to those claimed by the Tempests of the Eindhoven Wing, several were accounted for by the Tempests of No. 122 Wing, which had also been on patrol over the Ardennes from their forward base at Volkel – one of the few airfields ignored by the attackers – and more were destroyed over the Reichswald by the Spitfires of 126 Wing. The Spits of No. 131 Wing, returning from a dawn sweep, also intercepted fifty of the raiders over their base at St Denis-Westram and destroyed eighteen of them for no loss to themselves.

Anti-aircraft fire claimed a further 129 enemy fighter-bombers, bringing the total Luftwaffe loss for the operation to 226 aircraft, roughly a quarter of the attacking force. It was a loss that the Luftwaffe could scarcely afford, especially as most of the pilots who survived came down in Allied territory and were taken prisoner.

In the corridors of the German Air Ministry in Berlin, Operation Hermann was labelled as a huge success, and gave fuel to the enemy's struggling propaganda machine. But among the operational squadrons, there grew the conviction that the New Year's Day raid had been the Luftwaffe's swan-song, and that never again would the Germans be in a position to challenge the Allied air forces in strength.

In view of the situation, Yeoman had succeeded in postponing his departure on leave by ten days; longer than that, the group commander would not allow him. Nevertheless, it was clear that until aircraft reinforcements could be flown out from England, the handful of Tempests and Spitfires that had escaped the big attack would have to sustain the Allied air offensive – and that meant twice the amount of work for everyone involved.

During the first week of the New Year, the pilots of the Eindhoven Wing flew a minimum of two sorties a day, whenever the weather permitted, all of them low-level attacks on enemy transport and communications. In that week, the Wing lost seven aircraft and four pilots.

The mess at Eindhoven reassumed its former gloomy aspect. There were no social gatherings in the bar, and very little drinking by individuals. A pilot, his face betraying extreme fatigue, might wander in and swallow a hasty half-pint of beer before collapsing on his bed, but that was all. It was a situation that could not last for much longer.

Fortunately, the weather intervened. On the morning of 8 January it started to snow again, the blizzards accompanied by strong winds and abysmal temperatures. On both sides of the front, the struggle now was not so much to stay alive, as to stay warm.

At Rheine, its runways completely snowbound, Richter shuddered to think of the plight of the front-line soldiers, especially those on the crumbling eastern front. His adjutant, Hasso von Gleiwitz, had shown him a letter he had received from his brother, fighting somewhere in East Prussia; one paragraph stood out in Richter's mind, making his flesh crawl:

'If you actually saw me you would raise your hands in dismay. I am ragged and filthy. I have had the same underwear on for five weeks . . . if one doesn't get lice it's a miracle. If only the war were over soon; it has lasted long enough already.'

Too long, Richter thought. Best to end it now, in the misery of winter, so that with the coming of spring and its warmth we shall have fresh heart to start rebuilding out of the ruins we have created. Then, more realistically, he knew that the coming of spring would bring only more offensives, more slaughter, which would end only when Germany was a sea of ashes from frontier to frontier.

Johnny Schumacher came to see him one day, his face ashen and his hand trembling. In his hand he held a telegram; it was from his mother. He thrust it out for Richter to read, and the latter gave a gasp of astonishment.

Schumacher's father had been arrested.

It took Richter and his adjutant nearly two days of intensive enquiries before they could tell the distraught Schumacher why it had happened. His father had been arrested by the Gestapo for harbouring a Jew, a former schoolteacher.

'But I knew that old man,' Schumacher protested in bewilderment. 'He was gentle, and kind – a friend of my father's for many years. He wouldn't have hurt a fly.'

Richter stared at him and said nothing. They both knew that in such cases it was useless to protest.

Three days later came the news that Schumacher's father had died 'of a heart attack, while in police custody'. And shortly afterwards, an order arrived instructing Schumacher to report immediately to Gestapo HQ in Berlin. It was, the order said, merely a formality; his mother had been held for questioning, and his signature was needed for her release.

Richter tried to reassure him, but there was little he could do to lift his friend's deep depression. Wordlessly, Schumacher went off to his room, ostensibly to pack a bag.

An hour later, Richter was sitting in his office, moodily studying the latest situation reports, when he was startled by the sudden roar of an aero-engine. He got up and crossed quickly to the window; outside, flurries of snow swirled down through a thick mist.

He was just in time to see the vague shape of a Focke-Wulf, taking off into the murk. Furiously, he summoned von Gleiwitz from the outer office.

'Find out who that is,' he ordered. 'No one has been authorized to fly today. I want that aircraft back immediately, before the pilot breaks his neck!'

He turned back to the window, frowning, and heard his adjutant speaking rapidly on the telephone. Suddenly, von Gleiwitz's voice was drowned by the prolonged screech of an aircraft diving under full power.

Richter never saw the Focke-Wulf plummet out of the clouds. But he could not escape seeing the brilliant flash of the explosion, over on the far side of the airfield, or the dark smoke that burgeoned up into the foggy sky.

The coffin lay on the frozen ground beside the open grave in Rheine's little cemetery. The officers of Jagdgeschwader 66 stood with bowed heads as the chaplain read the funeral service. A watery sun shone down on the scene.

The chaplain ceased his murmuring, and Richter stepped forward. Looking straight ahead, as though surveying the rooks in the distant, barren tree-tops, he said:

'Major Schumacher was my friend. He was also a warrior in the finest traditions of Germany. Together, we fought long and bitter campaigns, and never once did he falter in his duty or his determination.' For the first time, he looked directly at the assembled officers, who stared woodenly in front of them. 'A few days ago, Major Schumacher received the tragic news that his father had died in the hands of the Gestapo.'

Behind Richter, Hasso von Gleiwitz stiffened, his eyes fearful; it was not good to say such things.

'However,' Richter continued, 'I do not wish it to be thought that this had any bearing on today's unhappy events. On his last flight, Major Schumacher was carrying out a weather check, which I personally authorized. His death was an accident.'

There was a noticeable flicker of true understanding in the eyes of several of the assembled officers, and Richter nodded slowly. It was good that they should understand.

There remained one last act to be performed. Reaching down, Richter removed the Nazi flag, with its large black swastika, that was draped over Schumacher's coffin, and reached out his hand to von Gleiwitz. The adjutant passed him another flag, reverently folded; it was the flag of Imperial Germany, and no crooked cross defaced it.

Gently, Richter unfurled it and spread it over the remains of his friend. Then he straightened up, saluted, and signalled to the firing party to carry on.

The salutes crashed out, sending the rooks wheeling and cawing in startled panic. The coffin was lowered into the grave and Richter, his heart leaden, heard the dull thud as clods of frozen earth fell upon it. He turned and strode away, followed by his offficers. As he walked on, the swastika flag slipped gradually from his hand, as though by accident, and lay crumpled in the snow. No one bothered to pick it up.

MOSQUITO SQUADRON
by Robert Jackson

SUMMER 1943 . . .

The Battle of Germany has begun. By night and day, RAF and USAAF bombers drive deep into enemy territory, striking at the heart of Germany's war effort . . .

But the Luftwaffe's fighter defences are stronger than ever before, and the loss of skilled airmen is appalling. To protect the bombers, the RAF forms a long-range fighter force and equips it with fast, powerful de Havilland Mosquitos. The spearhead of the Allied bombers support is to be the newest Mosquito Squadron, commanded by Squadron Leader George Yeoman . . .

HURRICANE SQUADRON
by Robert Jackson

MAY 1940

To Sergeant George Yeoman, cruising high above France in his Hurricane fighter, on his way to join his first operational squadron, the war seemed a million miles away. But at that very moment, the squadrons of the Luftwaffe were gathering to strike the first devastating blow in Hitler's Blitzkrieg on the Western front . . .

HURRICANE SQUADRON –

The story of a fighter squadron at war; of a handful of pilots struggling desperately against hopeless odds; of a young man's rise from the innocence of peace to the experience of war.

LIQUIDATE PARIS
by Sven Hassel

From the wartorn steppes of Russia, from the slopes of Monte Cassino, the stunned, bloody remnants of Hitler's armies were gathered to fight the last battle of the German Reich – the battle of the Western Front. And as the Allies advanced upon Paris, the war erupted into its most ruthless, most savage and cruel phase. Across the scarred, corpse-strewn landscape of northern France, the men of the panzer tank corps retreated – fighting a suicide action as they went . . .

0 552 11414 6 £1.50

SS GENERAL
by Sven Hassel

The 27th Panzers in Hitler's Penal Regiment had fought through the winter in the hell-hole that was Stalingrad. Now there were few survivors from the last massive Russian attack. Weary and nauseated by the horrors they'd seen on the Russian front, they crawled into a bunker near the banks of the Volga. Hunger, they had discovered, was more demoralising than fear or defeat. Then the brutal SS general arrived . . .

0 552 11317 4 £1.75

633 SQUADRON: OPERATION CRUCIBLE
by Frederick E. Smith

AUTUMN 1943:

A vindictive press campaign in the States had placed the blame for heavy U.S. losses over Europe on lack of support from the RAF. To restore American confidence – and guarantee the supply of B.17s to Europe – joint special operations were planned by RAF and 8th Air Force top brass, calling in 633 Squadron, whose Rhine Maiden mission had won them a shining reputation. Operation Crucible was to be a Dieppe-style landing launched by the Americans, and 633 Squadron were assigned their most hazardous role yet – giving ground support to the troops against totally unforeseen odds . . .

0 552 10741 7 80p

633 SQUADRON: OPERATION VALKYRIE
by Frederick E. Smith

The memory of Operation Vesuvius – the successful but suicidal attack on the Black Fjord – still haunted 633 Squadron. For there were those who could remember how, on a cold July morning in 1943, only a single crippled Mosquito had finally made it home . . . But now, barely a year later, it seemed as if the nightmare of that fateful mission would have to be lived through again. The Germans were once more processing the secret 'element' known as IMI – and were about to move their stocks from Norway into the safe heartland of Germany. If successful, the manoeuvre could turn the tide of war . . . For 633 Squadron it meant another 'impossible' mission; but it also meant a flight into the dark, unforgotten past . . .

0 552 11075 2 £1.50